Search for ELISE

ALISON TRIMPER

Published in Australia by Sid Harta Books & Print Pty Ltd,
ABN: 34632585293
23 Stirling Crescent, Glen Waverley, Victoria 3150 Australia
Telephone: +61 3 9560 9920, Facsimile: +61 3 9545 1742
E-mail: author@sidharta.com.au

First published in Australia 2023
This edition published 2024
Copyright © Alison Trimper 2023

Cover design, typesetting: WorkingType (www.workingtype.com.au)

Disclaimer: *Search for Elise* is a work of fiction. Characters, their names, their
businesses and the events and incidents involving them are the products of the
author's imagination. Any resemblance to actual persons, living or dead, or
actual events is purely coincidental.

Alison Trimper
Search for Elise
ISBN: 978-1-922958-61-7

ABOUT THE AUTHOR

Alison Trimper has enjoyed a lifelong fascination with words – writing short stories, compiling family anecdotes, and writing stories for children. *Search for Elise* is her second novel and is set in rural New South Wales, as is her first novel, *Divine Hayfields*. She gathered her  understanding of rural life growing up on the family farm near Glen Innes, New South Wales. Alison and her husband farmed tea trees on the mid-north coast of New South Wales. She then became a mature-age student and completed her education degree, followed by a Masters in Special Education. Alison greatly enjoyed her years teaching and consistently reminded her students that words, when correctly used, can paint pictures just as detailed and evocative as artists' mediums.

Alison is now retired and lives with her husband on the outskirts of Toowoomba. Her three adult sons and their families are frequent visitors. Alison enjoys cooking for large family gatherings and the leisurely conversation-filled meals that follow. She also enjoys bushwalking and watercolour painting.

ALSO BY THE AUTHOR

Divine Hayfields

DEDICATION

*In memory of my dear older brother
who was so encouraging, but sadly didn't
get to read the end results.*

ACKNOWLEDGEMENTS

During the writing of this book, I spoke to more professional people than friends about details and ideas. I asked specific questions. I would like to thank all of those professional people who cheerfully engaged with my questions and, without realising, helped me clarify my thoughts. Special thanks to certain members of the Queensland Police Force, Rural Fire Brigade, and to several nurses for their willingly given, professional advice and suggestions.

Thank you to my wonderful husband who put up with no conversation, late dinners, and provided whisky when my frown grew too big.

Thank you to Glenda, Rowan, Jennifer and Charlie for cheerfully agreeing to read, pick up mistakes and make suggestions.

My thanks also go to my editor, who patiently dealt with my still-very-evident inexperience in the publishing field.

CHARACTERS

Elise Dean, Private Investigator
Detective Sergeant Kaylee Bradshaw, Muswellbrook Police
Detective Senior Constable Ben Wharton,
Muswellbrook Police

The Lardner family
Nathan, deceased, owned tattoo parlours
Cleo, 47, his widow
Hadley, 27, their son, university dropout
Sophia, 25, their daughter, nurse
Tobias, 22, their son, small-time drug dealer
Lex, 21, university student

The Nester family
Evander, 49, fences stolen goods
Rhea, 42, his wife
Damien, 23, their son, runs garage owned by his father that
rebirths stolen cars
Christos, 21, their son, spray painter, works with Damien
Karah, 19, their daughter, university student

THE DEAN FAMILY

Bill, 60, trucking company dispatcher

Sharon, 57, his wife, typist, Burt Bunrack's sister

Brad, 37, their son, cousin of Silvio Bunrack

Rebecca, 35, cousin of Silvio Bunrack, married to Ted
Buckley; children, Mike, Lily and Jonty

Elise, 29, private investigator, cousin of Silvio Bunrack,
business partner of Diego Bannerman

THE BUCKLEY FAMILY

Graham, farmer, lives near Wheeler

Jan, his wife, leather worker

Ted, married to Rebecca, sister of Elise Dean

Twin sons currently overseas

THE BANNERMAN FAMILY

Pat, 51, owns a carpentry business

Emilia, 48, his wife, nurse

Diego, 29, private investigator, business partner of Elise

Mick, truck driver

Mr and Mrs Carlton

Their two sons Snake (Eric) and Feral (Patrick) Carlton
work for Damien Nester, rebirthing stolen cars.

CHAPTER 1

A tranquil evening, that's all she wanted! Elise Dean stretched luxuriously. *Oh, what a day, what a terribly long day it's been!* She took a sip of Pinot Grigio and admired her shoes, turning her ankles from side to side. She hadn't been able to wear these beautiful smoke-blue suede stilettos to work. She'd strained her back that morning, so she was rebelliously wearing the cherished shoes now, on the lounge, where they wouldn't hurt her to walk. *Yes, indeed they looked mighty fine.* She had another mouthful of the prawn salad she'd picked up on the way home, not because she was still hungry but because it was so tasty. Another sip of wine, another glance at her lovely shoes, and she was finally relaxed.

Now at last the day was done. Nothing more could go wrong. She was home, she could relax. Although it was only early evening, Elise had almost succumbed to sleep on the lounge, when she felt a cool draught across the back of her neck, breaking her reverie and making her shiver a little.

Without warning, she was grabbed from behind, arms pinned to her side. She struggled, knocking over the coffee table. The wine glass shattered on the floor. Prawn salad and phone went flying. She caught a glimpse of a black-clad body. Rough arms reached around and stretched duct tape over her mouth. A second strip was quickly placed across her eyes. She was yanked to her feet, hands dragged behind her back. Elise heard the plastic *zziipp* of cable ties being pulled tight around her wrists. She heard her front door being thrown open.

Furiously, Elise twisted and writhed. Her attacker shoved her out through the door. She was dragged rather than carried along her short front path, fighting desperately to get free. Out in the street, she felt herself lifted by rough hands. She wriggled and kicked, felt one of her beautiful shoes come off, heard it hit the road. Her mind whirled. She was dumped unceremoniously onto the cold metal floor of a delivery van. She heard the doors slam shut. As she lay, winded, she felt the van take off and accelerate around the corner, down the street, away from her beloved safe-haven home. Her heart sank in despair as she fought vainly against being thrown about like flotsam in the back of the racing vehicle. She heard one of the men tell the other one to slow down.

'Don't want to get done for speeding with this load, Snake!'

'Yeah, you've got a point.'

'How'd you find out where she lived so quickly?'

'Easy. They've got a little hack at work. You just feed in a name and it spits out rego, address, license; pretty much everything except shoe size.'

'That's handy but not standard issue for a garage, is it?'

'Nah.'

'So, what do they use it for?'

Snake felt like he was on shaky ground. 'Can't really say.' He changed the subject to divert Tobias. 'What are we doing with her, Tobe?'

'I guess we'll have to knock her off. Too much trouble with explanations if she turns up alive somewhere.'

'Well, how do we get rid of her after we do her in?'

'Easy. Go out Hartseig Road, past the ruins of the old Hartseig church. You know where that is?' Eyes on the road, Tobias didn't see Snake shake his head. 'You'll see a farmer has pushed up piles of logs, waiting for them to dry out enough to burn. I had to go out past there one day with Hadley to see a man about a dog.' He grimaced at the memory. 'Some jackasses live in the country that's for sure! Anyway, all we have to do is chuck her body on one of those piles and throw a few more logs on her. The farmer won't suspect anything. He'll just throw in a match one day and *voila!* We're rid of her.'

Despite being tossed about as the vehicle cornered, the hairs on the back of Elise's neck rose. She shuddered in horror, not just at the idea of her death, but at the very casual way he spoke about killing her. She had to escape, but her hands were tied. *I must make a plan, something, anything,* she thought desperately. *I don't suppose they'll waste time feeding me if they are going to kill me.* She had no idea where she was heading, racking her brain for any recollection of Hartseig Road. She faintly remembered something about a road with that name, but in her jangled state, the knowledge floated just outside her memory.

She couldn't see a thing with her eyes taped shut and had no hope of trying to memorise turns in the road because she was being thrown about so much. Elise realised that panicking was dangerous. *Must try to stay calm.*

To distract herself from the horror of the unknown and her helplessness, Elise forced her mind to do a detailed recap of her day. *Who knows? Some detail from today might give me a clue about what's happening now.*

Just before this violent invasion, she was deeply enjoying being home. She was not an antisocial woman, far from it. She had many friends from school, university, and various jobs. She was often out enjoying their company any night of the week. She loved her extended family, frequently enjoying a pub dinner and catch up with her brother. She was no stranger to her cousin's family, happily playing with her cousin's baby when they were in town. She also enjoyed relaxing weekend visits to their home at the horse stud, Divine Hayfields, where her cousin and his wife worked.

Tonight though, had been a welcome relief to kick back at home and switch off her brain. She relished the cosy nest that was her home – a tiny, detached house in the township of Muswellbrook which serviced a thriving rural community.

Elise tried to ignore what was happening to her by thinking about her recent life. *So what if I'm paying an enormous amount to the bank each month?* Her home was her domain, where she could shut out the world and just chill.

Despite the overdraft, Elise truly enjoyed her independence, her little home on the street corner, and her tiny backyard. In some spots, it was hard to tell exactly where her yard ended, and the back lane began. The fence was dilapidated, broken in places and non-existent in others. Elise didn't rate as a home handywoman, so the fence was still on her 'to do' list. In the yard, there was enough space for a pull-out clothesline, and she liked to put a deck chair under it on sunny weekends. A short walk led into the kitchen through the spacious laundry that doubled as a garden shed. As well as holding the usual washing machine and dryer, it had room to stow her portable barbeque and the odd gardening tool, not that she used those much, but she liked having them. Through the kitchen, vivid with matching red appliances, into the living room, the deep, soft leather lounge stretched across the long wall facing the bedroom and bathroom doors, the television mounted on the wall between them. Large plush colourful cushions and throw rugs filled the floor space. Immediately on the left after leaving the kitchen was the compact bathroom. Elise's bedroom was comfortably fitted with a queen bed and a second smaller television on the wall above the cluttered dressing table. Her bedroom also had French doors leading out to a very small balcony that looked onto the tree-lined street. The second bedroom with double bed and antique chest of drawers was perfectly adequate for the odd sleep-over guest, usually a school friend who had too many drinks to drive home safely. That was the total of her cherished domain: not big, but hers!

Carefully, Elise let the events of the day roll through her head in summary. It was hard not to lose the thread because she was being banged around so much in the van. But she felt it was important to keep her mind focused on something that wouldn't increase her anxiety level. First thing that day, she had stepped half asleep into the shower, tripping on the small plinth. She'd grabbed awkwardly at the tap to stop herself falling. Wrenched her back.

Then the blow dryer turned her hair into a crow's nest. She gave up on appearances, dressed down in jeans and an emerald-green sweatshirt with safe, flat shoes. Impossible to wear stilettos with a wrenched back. She'd wandered into her kitchen, expecting the vivid red appliances to cheer her up, but they failed her that morning. She had looked for a coffee re-boot. The milk came out of the carton in lumps. She'd binned it in disgust, threw down a couple of painkillers and slammed out of the house. As she left, Elise had reflected that it was just as well she didn't have a pet. On a morning like that, it would surely have bitten her!

With a system deprived of a coffee hit, Elise struggled

with the tide of other workers as she drove to her office. The main inland north-south highway ran through the centre of town and was currently undergoing a major upgrade. Several detours were in place making navigating to the small business centre a headache for locals and visitors alike. Contrary traffic, pedestrians and some just plain idiots slowed her little red hatchback to a crawl. Frustration was building as she halted at yet another stop sign held up by a bored youth. *BANG*, she was rear-ended. The savage jerk didn't do her back or her temper any good.

'Sorry, sorry, sorry,' the driver sobbed. 'My boyfriend just dumped me by TEXT!' The last word was uttered in a disbelieving screech. Elise bit her tongue. Hard. *No point in making matters worse by stating the obvious like what are you doing reading messages when you're supposed to be driving a car?* Elise consoled herself with the thought that the young woman's insurance would be paying, not hers, so one way or another, the driver would eventually feel the pain Elise was feeling right now.

'Okay, okay. Relax, calm down.' Elise hoped she sounded halfway sympathetic. Miraculously, while everyone else was stuck, a tow truck made its way through to the little drama. The front of the other car was extensively mashed in, but all that was really wrong with Elise's little hatchback was that the hatchback latch was broken. She mentally shrugged, *I'll get it fixed when I get around to it.* She collected the sniffling driver's details and left her to the mercies of the tow-truck driver.

So started a bad day for Elise Dean. She was twenty-nine years old, single, and co-owned a private investigating firm. Elise's dad, Bill, was Australian from way back, probably the first convict ship. Sharon, Elise's mum, had emigrated from England with her older brother Burt Bunrack and the rest of her family when she was in her late teens. She had been a typist in the office of the transport company Bill worked for in the town of Muswellbrook where they both lived.

It was a thriving country centre servicing mine workers from the coal mines to the east of town and farmers to the west of town. The farms were mainly running beef cattle, some sheep, or were horse studs. Bill had wooed Sharon and she was happy to embrace the package that was marriage back then. They had a son, Brad, a daughter, Rebecca, and then a considerable time later, Elise. As a result of the age difference, half the time Elise was ignored by her siblings and the other half, she was ridiculously spoilt. As a family, they got along in a casually happy way, not intruding much in each other's lives but always available when called on for celebrations or commiserations. Sharon and Bill both expressed misgivings about Elise's chosen career path but Brad and Bec were supportive in an indulgent way.

At work at last, Elise had parked out the back and staggered up the fire stairs, trying to be easy on her back.

Juggling her bag, water bottle and phone, she stepped into the office of Abbey Inc. The first thing she saw was Diego scowling at some documents. She knew that face and quickly made herself scarce, hunkering down behind her desk and firing up her laptop. Occasionally, Diego got a curly problem or was stumped by some red tape. When that happened, his thick dark brows came down making his face look like a thunderbolt. At these times, Elise avoided him, leaving him alone to sort out his problem. Usually, his sharp brain found a solution and his carefree nature promptly reasserted itself.

With Diego already engrossed in work, Elise quietly made a start on her own tasks. Her current investigation was a bit ticklish. She'd been hired by a prominent family man, Evander Nester, with known criminal associations, to investigate another shady family, the Lardners, with similar criminal associations because of the blossoming romance between the Nester daughter and one of the Lardner sons. When taking on the case, she had mused how strange it was that as they all worked mostly on the wrong side of the law, they would have no problem pooling their resources through a convenient marriage. However, Elise was discovering a lot of unsavoury information that would soon have her puzzling over whether to go to the police with what she uncovered.

Tossing about in the van, her head began to ache, matching the pain in her back. Elise gave up trying to figure out whether there had been any hint during the day that this would happen to her this evening.

✳ ✳ ✳

As the men slammed the van doors, across the road from Elise's house, Mavis Wells stared open-mouthed from behind the net curtains in her living room. *What the heck?* She had watched her fair share of television dramas and knew trouble when she saw it. *That poor lass is being taken!* At last, her careful attention to the comings and goings in her street had paid off.

In her fifty-third year, Mavis was no stranger to her mobile phone. She quickly grabbed it and pressed triple zero. In the pause before she was connected, she tried to marshal her thoughts. She could hardly believe what she'd witnessed. Then she mentally kicked herself. *Damn, I didn't even get the number plate!*

CHAPTER 2

In the police station, Detective Sergeant Kaylee Bradshaw shuffled papers, half-heartedly catching up on some filing. She was bored and restless. *Why are Tuesdays always so quiet?*

Her attention sharpened with the ringing of the phone on her desk.

'Yes Dispatch? What have you got for me?'

'We've had a call that a girl has been kidnapped. Clement Street, number twenty. The neighbour over the road saw it happen, said the girl was struggling but was thrown in the back of a van.'

Kaylee quickly took down the details, feeling her adrenalin rising. As she ended the call, Kaylee swivelled her chair to scan the room for another available officer. Her eyes landed on Ben Wharton, Detective Senior Constable. His local knowledge, both rural and in town made him a valuable partner and they were an effective team, with a string of successful police operations behind them. With a sincere smile, she beckoned him urgently. She enjoyed working with him, liked his attitude and attention to detail. She watched the tall officer walk easily over to her desk.

'Ben! We're out of here NOW! The lull is over. We've had a report from a lady, says she witnessed a kidnapping. Let's go investigate! Hurry.' Kaylee stood as she spoke, pocketing her phone and slinging her bag strap over her shoulder.

Ben Wharton spun on his toes, grabbed his jacket and keys, and spoke over his shoulder, 'I'll drive. You fill me in.'

In the deepening twilight of the long summer evening, Ben steered efficiently while listening to Kaylee speculate on what was ahead of them.

'Our caller identified herself as Mavis. Lucky for us daylight saving meant Mavis could still see the action. The streets round here aren't exactly well lit. You know, Ben, it's a good thing there are a few honest-to-goodness busybodies around. If it weren't for them, we'd never find things out. Let's hope our Mavis was an observant busybody. Here! Turn right here.'

Turning into Clement Street, the first thing their headlights picked up was one blue stiletto in the middle of the road. It was outside a house from which light spilled through the open front door.

'You go and see what you can find out from inside that open front door. I'll have a chat to Mavis. Come back to me in five,' Kaylee delegated. She registered Ben's sarcastic, 'Yes, boss,' and grinned. She knew that smart mouth wouldn't stop his strong powers of observation and attention to the job at hand.

She stepped briskly from the police vehicle and strode up

the path of number 21, opposite 20. She had barely raised her hand to knock when Mavis whipped her front door open. 'My, you got here quick. Come in! Come in!'

'Okay, Mavis.' Kaylee kept her voice low, and her words slow, knowing that often had a calming effect on excited members of the public. 'Let's just sit down and I'll ask you a few questions. No need to rush. I have an officer checking out the house over the road. If this is a kidnapping, you've helped us get onto it very quickly.' Kaylee also knew that flattery helped ensure greater levels of co-operation from volunteer witnesses, although it sometimes encouraged them to exaggerate. She prided herself on her ability to spot embellishments.

Mavis allowed herself a brief proud smirk and then poured out an excited jumble of words. 'Oh Detective! That poor girl's been kidnapped. I saw it! Lucky I was looking out the window just then. Right in front of my eyes! One of her pretty shoes fell off. Blue it was. She always dresses smartly, that girl. Probably broken, now. The shoe, I mean. They shoved her in the back, fighting and kicking like a cornered cat. I don't mean shoved her in her back, they threw her in the back. It was a van. She's not very big. But she's gone! They just slammed those back doors and raced off. Driving far too fast to be safe in these streets, think of the children!'

Mentally, Kaylee rolled her eyes. 'What was the van like, Mavis? Could you tell me the number plate?'

Mavis gave an exaggerated groan. 'No! I was so stunned.

I felt so sorry for that poor girl. I just forgot to notice the number plate. I'm sorry.'

'Not to worry. Can you describe the vehicle? Was there anything special that made it stand out to you?'

Kaylee had mustered her patience and was making a determined effort to calmly glean as much information as possible from Mavis. Out in the street, Ben pulled on gloves, then bent and picked up the shoe. *This is brand new*, he noted. He dropped it in a plastic bag and walked up the front path of Elise's house.

'Anybody home? Hello? I'm Senior Constable Wharton. Hello?'

Silence greeted him. Standing at the front door, Ben took in the overturned table, the scattered food, the phone, the broken glass, and the babbling television. The scene didn't have the look of someone just going out for an impulsive joy ride. He could see across the lounge room into the kitchen. On the bench he saw a bright red toaster and matching coffee machine. He screwed up his face. *How could you face that much red first thing in the morning? Ah well, each to his or her own, I guess!* He focused his gaze, trying to ignore all the red appliances, and spotted a large leather tote bag. *So, not a robbery, either*, he guessed.

He quickly but carefully scanned all he could see inside the lounge room. His nose told him this was not the home of a pet owner, nor the home of a smoker. The room had a clean airy smell combined with recently spilled prawn salad. *Someone had also had a glass of wine (or two?).* The overturned table spoke of a struggle. *How did the intruder get in?*

He heard movement behind him and turned. 'You finished with Mavis already?' he asked Kaylee in surprise. 'How'd you get on?'

'Not spectacularly well. She saw the woman struggling, so not a girl as she said when she called it in, and being dragged from the house by a masked man in black. Her hands appeared to be tied behind her back and one of her shoes fell off. A second man, also masked, helped the first to throw the victim into the back of a van. They drove off at speed. Unfortunately, our Mavis didn't get the number plate. She said it was a new-looking white van, just like any of the vans you see every day.' Kaylee's voice dropped disgustedly. She continued, 'Mavis says the woman is a private investigator but can't recall the name of the outfit, doesn't know whether it was a one-woman business or not. Knows her name is Elise but not her surname. What does this scene tell you?'

'I think we should call Clicks and Paul in to do a forensic investigation. Clearly, there has been some sort of struggle in the lounge room. There's a mobile phone on the floor, so not a robbery. It looks like her handbag is still in the kitchen, ditto on robbery. And I don't know any woman who'd go out for a drive without her handbag! I didn't go in, will leave it to

Forensics to check out first. I have a hunch our abductors, if that's what they are, came in through the back.'

Kaylee felt her pulse quicken as she made the call requesting the forensic team. She had a sincere respect for Ben's hunches. His brain worked in some quirky ways, but his instinct was seldom off the mark.

'Sounds interesting. What say you and I zip around the back for a bit of a look-see while we wait for Clicks and Paul.'

'Clicks and Paul' were Jenny Mumford and Dave Hogan, the police forensic team. Jenny was a short, cheerful woman originally from England. She was highly skilled in the field of forensic photography, but no amount of talent could prevent the application of such an obvious nickname as 'Clicks'. She didn't mind the nickname, to her it meant that she was an accepted part of the team. She worked well with her partner, Dave Hogan (commonly known as Paul), and often grinned to herself about their names. So typical in Australia to have funny or off-beat nicknames.

The two tall police officers followed the street round the corner and entered the dusty lane that ran behind the row of houses.

'What did Mavis say about the van? Was it waiting out the front all the time? Or did it pull up as the woman was dragged out?'

'She said it was out the front. So, I'd hazard a guess the attacker was dropped off at the laneway, if that's how they accessed the house, and then the driver took the van round the front to wait. Seems a bit risky as far as witnesses to the action, taking her out in the street. I'd have thought this laneway was a better option for secrecy. But then again, apparently it was all very quick.'

'Watch where you're putting your feet, hard to tell what's in this rubbishy grass. Couldn't really call this mess a back fence, could you? Shine your torch over here, can you? But let's not go any closer. Look! Two clear footprints going into the yard. We'd better let Clicks and Paul know there's work for them to do here as well. I think we can safely say I was right about how the house was accessed.'

'Okay. You can crow now, but don't get too cocky. You haven't solved the case yet, you know.'

They headed back the way they'd come. The banter masked their serious attitude to the job at hand but revealed an easy working relationship. They'd been the senior detectives at the station for some time now, and enjoyed their work together. They each respected the skills of the other and set a fine example of law enforcement and solving crimes for the more junior or less experienced officers in the station.

CHAPTER 3

A few streets away, Diego Bannerman strode into his third-floor apartment, throwing his satchel strap over the hook on the hat rack in the entry. His Irish dad, Pat, fell for his Spanish mother, Emilia, while he was on an adventure holiday participating in the running of the bulls in Spain. Of course, he was injured and wound up in hospital, and of course, Emilia was his nurse! They emigrated to Australia to begin their life together. Diego was their only child, neither over-indulged nor neglected and he grew up to be an easy-going, intelligent adult. Except that right now, his patience was badly frazzled. *What a pig of a day!* All his efforts at work had simply led to more questions and no answers. He felt like he'd wasted the day. Now all he wanted was a quiet evening, undisturbed, where he could down a few beers and zone out watching a game on telly. His fierce frown said, 'Woe betide anyone who disturbs me!' He kicked off his boots and headed to the fridge.

Diego was Elise's business partner. Together, they owned a private investigation firm. They met at university – he was doing his master's degree in business administration, and

Elise was studying criminology. They had similar interests, similar off-beat senses of humour and similar laid-back attitudes. You could say they hit it off instantly and never looked back. They decided to go into business together about six years ago after each had been working various jobs and gaining experience in the adult world. They had chosen the business name Abbey Inc. so it would appear first in directories. The theory was that people looking for a private investigator would be too stressed to look further than the first listing. It seemed to work. Elise and Diego seldom had an empty job chart and their comfortable bank balance reflected this. Their promotional material described them as investigators of criminal and other cases. They worked for anyone who could afford their fees.

They were often hired by law firms for criminal background checks and by insurance companies for investigating suspicious claims. They did the legwork because those who hired them either had not the time or the manpower for the job. Abbey Inc. also did their share of investigating one or the other partner in divorce cases. With his business background, Diego enjoyed handling corporate work. Canny businessmen asked him to probe the backgrounds of companies to discover any risks linked to potential investment. Farmers sometimes asked for background checks on prospective employees. Sometimes, Abbey Inc. was asked by corporations to dig into the family history, criminal records, and employment history of a prospective employee. Diego and Elise often interviewed witnesses, relatives, and acquaintances of suspects and victims. Sometimes they were asked to observe crime suspects and report findings to the client.

Diego and Elise were kept busy all over the place looking into people from all walks, and more often than not, those people knew nothing about it. Occasionally, one of them appeared in court trials as an expert witness. Very occasionally, they grabbed suspects and criminals and released them to the police, rather than seeing them get away. One of the most interesting aspects of the job, in Elise's opinion, was when they were asked to investigate witnesses, relatives, suspects and victims. Often the information they uncovered was hilarious, sometimes tragic, but always requiring absolute discretion. She found the social element of their work totally absorbing because she was constantly surprised by human behaviours.

At the end of every investigation, Abbey Inc. was expected to write a report or case summary highlighting discoveries and findings. This was because their fees were eye-wateringly steep, and the clients always wanted a little (or a large) printed something to show for their money.

The *How to Be a Private Investigator* handbook recommended private investigators have a background in criminal justice, criminology, or law. It also mentioned discretion, honesty and tenacity as well as strong powers of observation. So, Diego and Elise were a perfect fit for their job.

They were usually hired solo but were always available to each other for discussion and consultation or simply a fresh perspective. Sometimes things went wrong with their search or surveillance, and they wound up in a spot of bother. In these cases, they usually tried to sort it out themselves. Their habit was to steer clear of the police unless it was an extreme emergency. They found that the more they stayed under the radar of the police, the easier their life was. Experience had taught them that they were undervalued by the police service, and they had quickly learned to keep themselves well separated from them.

Today, Diego had been working on a new investigation. The client had a business downtown and wanted Diego to investigate his neighbours, who he claimed were 'up to no good'. Diego had run into brick wall after brick wall and was gradually concluding that he was investigating some seriously bad people. When he had decided to try working backwards from his subject, for a different perspective, he found that his client also appeared to be underhand and secretive, to say the least. He wanted to run his ideas past Elise, but she had been in and out of the office all day. She also seemed out of sorts and preoccupied. Knowing her as well as he did, Diego had decided to wait for a more favourable time to consult with her. *Put it out of your head, maybe the picture will be clearer in the morning,* Diego told himself, finishing his beer.

Pushing himself up off the lounge, he padded into the kitchen for another beer and put a couple of slices of yesterday's pizza in the microwave. Intelligent he may be, but he failed to see how putting energy into food preparation made any sense at all.

With beer in hand and his reheated pizza on a plate, Diego made himself comfortable on the lounge. Just as he filled his mouth with hot pizza, his phone buzzed. *What now?*

'Hello, this is Diego Bannerman.' His words were slightly muffled by pizza.

'This is Detective Senior Constable Ben Wharton from Muswellbrook police.'

Swallowing quickly, Diego mentally scanned current and past cases that might mean a call from the police.

'What can I do for you?'

'Is your partner Elise Dean?'

'Yes, Elise Dean is my business partner.'

It was Diego's habit, developed as his experience with private investigation grew, to give concise answers but not to give out any information that wasn't specifically sought. He waited for the policeman to come to the point of his call.

'Do you know her whereabouts?' As a skilled police investigator, it was Ben's habit also not to reveal anything more than was strictly necessary.

'No.'

Damn, we could be hedging around each other all night, Ben thought with a wry grin.

'We had a call to her address earlier this evening, a disturbance. Found the place open, in a state of disorder, but no Elise. Worryingly, her handbag and purse were on the kitchen bench and there were no signs of anything being stolen. Mobile phone on the floor. Does she have a car?'

Diego felt his stomach tighten. *What the heck?* 'She drives a red hatchback. Did you see it there?'

'Hmm, yes, her car was there. Sorry to disrupt your evening, but can I come round and get some details from you? Easier than on the phone.' Ben kept his tone friendly, almost casual.

'Sure. Apartment three, Koenga Beacons, Pelton Court. Press the buzzer.'

'Right. Thanks for that. My partner and I will be there in about fifteen minutes.'

Ben ended the call, started the police car and chuckled.

'Well? Share!' Kaylee demanded.

'He's a PI and we're detectives. Unless we can get him onside straight away, it's going to be a real circus getting him to open up with us!'

'Surely he will care enough about his partner's disappearance to be completely cooperative,' Kaylee spoke reproachfully.

'Yeah, I guess you've got a point.'

They were both absorbed in their own thoughts as Ben drove across town. Arriving at Pelton Court, the detectives followed Diego's instructions and pressed the buzzer. In a short time, they were seated in Diego's lounge room; introductions were made and they started work.

Diego was alarmed at the story the detectives told but he was mystified as well. He said he and Elise didn't always immediately share what they were working on. Depending on how simple or complex their current jobs were, sometimes there was no consultation between them at all. He knew nothing about the case Elise was working on.

After some questions and answers, the detectives felt they were really no further on. Diego fidgeted with a hangnail for a bit, then said hesitantly, 'I know it is usual to ask for information from the public in cases like this, especially since it seems so clear cut that Elise has been kidnapped, but I'd rather we held off on that.'

'Why?' Ben thought it a strange request.

'Well, you know what we do. A lot of our success lies in us remaining as anonymous and faceless as possible. Pretty sure if we go putting pictures of Elise in the paper and on the news, there will go her chances of staying unknown. That'll be a big disadvantage for her future work.'

'Good point,' Ben conceded, 'but how do you think her family will feel about that? Won't they be wanting us to pull out all the stops to get her back?'

'Could you suggest they stay away from publicity for a bit? If they aren't keen, let me know and I'll try to persuade them. They're sensible down-to-earth people, very nice.'

'Okay, we'll be talking to them in the morning. Will let you know how we get on. And Diego, in return for us keeping this out of the public eye, can you leave it to us to do the investigation?'

'I'm not sure I follow your reasoning.'

'It's really about the procedures we follow. I don't want us wasting time on something you've already done. I don't want information overlooked because you don't think it's important and we do. Do you follow me?'

'Yeah, I get you.'

'On the other hand, if you *do* hear anything or think of anything that might be helpful, please don't hesitate to call me or Kaylee.'

Since Diego was unable to add much more to their investigation, they left him and called it a night.

CHAPTER 4

Cleo Lardner leaned against the wall in her front hall as she took off her sneakers. *Wow, this life of making my own decisions is exhilarating but tiring.* After such a busy day, she was looking forward to a relaxing evening. What bliss to have the house to herself. She briefly wondered if she should pace herself a little better, and not fill every day to the brim relishing her freedom to choose where she went, what she did and how long she did it for. She also realised she must keep time every day to work at her growing business. How she loved her new-found independence. She pushed herself off the wall, peeled off her gym clothes and headed towards her immaculate bathroom. Although she was tired, she enjoyed the feeling of a job well done. *I'm getting fitter every day, looking less and less like a mother of four in her forties,* she thought, pleased.

In the warm bubble bath, she smoothed her hands over her flat stomach, enjoying the soapy water on her skin. She idly doodled in the bubbles that slid down her thigh. Her mind drifted back over the years. Every memory was still crystal clear. She had fallen for Nathan when she was nineteen. He was loud and opinionated, took control of everything and seemed so powerful. As a naïve and over-protected teenager with parents who showed little affection, it was easy to decide his loudness meant he'd be able to take care of her. She thought it would be a wonderful relationship with him taking responsibility for everything, including her. She would be safe and happy. She was very immature. They were married when she was twenty. Cleo soon discovered that Nathan being loud and opinionated when on dates in public equated with him being overbearing, domineering and downright controlling at home. He frequently and forcefully gave her his opinions of her friends and every opinion was negative. Cleo learned quite quickly not to invite her friends to the house when Nathan was at home.

He began to restrict her visits out, as well as being unpleasant enough to deter her friends from calling. She had to account for every hour of every day, and he loudly condemned any time she spent having coffee or lunch with girlfriends. She quickly learned not to argue, but to quietly comply. Gradually she reduced her time with friends because it was easier to do that than live through his angry, repetitious tirades. Cleo was lonely. Bit by bit, it dawned on her that although Nathan demanded to know every detail of who she saw and what she did, he was very reticent about his business.

She had asked him one day about their apparent wealth and he had responded dismissively, 'tyche', which she knew to mean 'luck'. She had often heard him use that word, but he didn't explain any further what he meant by 'luck'.

Tentatively she raised the idea of starting a family. To her surprise, Nathan agreed. In a short time, she was the mother of a son, then a daughter, then two more sons. She was busy. She adored her children and showered them with the love she'd not received as a child. She played with them, shopped for them, cooked for them. But when she suggested joining a playgroup for the children, Nathan put his foot down. He demanded she stay at home with the children, only going out to shop for them and for household supplies. He phoned her at odd times, both on the home line and her mobile. She knew he was checking up on her and she began to feel more isolated and lonelier for adult friendship.

One day, she had made a quick detour to a seedier section of town, before doing her grocery shopping. She was in search of a market she had heard of that had a wide variety of stalls selling toys and stationery that would amuse her beloved children. She had been surprised to see a tattoo parlour and recognised the name 'Tyche' gaudily emblazoned on the window.

That evening, she'd asked Nathan about the tattoo parlour, and he had flown into a rage. He shouted at her to mind her own business. It was his job to provide for his family, which he said he did very well, and it was not her business to ask him about it. After that, although she did not think a tattoo parlour would pay enough to keep them as comfortably as they lived, she was too afraid to ask him any more questions.

When the children started school, Cleo volunteered to assist in the school library and the canteen. Nathan grudgingly approved of these activities, but Cleo immediately discovered that developing friendships with other mothers was not negotiable from his point of view. She was not quite as lonely when she was at the school, but she sorely felt the lack of close female friends. She knew the other mothers thought her aloof, but she decided it was easier not to become friendly because inevitably Nathan would shut the process down. She knew that many people found him impatient and intolerant or worse. They were wary of him, fearing his explosive, abusively expressed opinions.

Cleo was not unintelligent, but she was unable to leave Nathan. She had no qualifications for employment, and she feared that if she did leave Nathan, he would find her. He would force her back home. Her life would be worse because he would increase the checking up and controlling. She decided to use her time in the school library and the canteen to learn some skills. Her aim was to eventually find a creative interest that she could use to earn an income. She wanted to begin an online business that she could build as a basis for an independent life after the children were grown and gone.

In the cooling bubble bath, she added hot water. Her mind skipped forward. The children were no longer children. Her oldest son, Hadley, was a worry. He had begun a pharmacy degree but had dropped out in his third year. He had a flat close to his brother, Tobias's flat, kept very odd hours and was surly and uncommunicative. Tobias had no job that Cleo knew of, but he never seemed short of money, driving the latest cars, and always dressed in quality clothes. Tobias had always been impulsive and irresponsible. Cleo shuddered to think what they were both up to. Her daughter, Sofia, was a nurse, living in the nurses' quarters in the big hospital where she worked. Lex, the baby of the family, shared a flat with a friend, a fellow university student. He was a quiet and hardworking young man, studying journalism. He gave Cleo none of the qualms caused by his older brothers.

After the children moved on to high school, Cleo had begun carefully and quietly developing a business creating unusual combinations of fruits and vegetables to make specialty jams, relishes, and chutneys. She advertised online and slowly built a solid client base. It was impossible to keep the growing business a secret from Nathan, but Cleo minimised its size and success when she spoke of it to him. He, in turn, sneered derisively about her 'little hobby' and laughed cruelly when she mentioned making up orders.

One day, Cleo had been feeling especially lonely and miserable. She had moped through the dishes, then turned from the sink and surveyed her workbench. Everything was laid out ready for her to make rhubarb, pear and garlic jam for an order for a café up the north coast. This combination was very popular at the Piglet Café because it teamed well with their specialty pork dishes and deli meats. They wanted twenty-four little pots for retail and a large catering-size jar for use in their kitchen. Cleo was excited to think that it wasn't just food outlets using her product, they were selling it to the public as well.

She began to fantasise about developing a multi-million-dollar business, imagining the delight she would feel shoving her success in Nathan's face. Her mood quickly soured as she thought of Nathan, but her surreal frame of mind persisted. She mechanically gathered the long pink rhubarb stalks into her hand and began savagely slicing. Normally very careful not to include the least little bit of the toxic leaves, Cleo viciously sliced right to the tip of the last leaf and threw the lot in the pot, paying no attention to the deadly leaf parts. Carefully, she completed cooking and bottling the jam. A sizeable serving wouldn't fit in the last jar. She calmly set it aside in a dish for use at home.

Suddenly her dreamlike calm evaporated as she heard Nathan's car in the driveway. He hustled in with his usual blustering noise, cursing about the rotten traffic and demanding a whisky and soda. He seemed not to even notice the large round jar of jam and the neat line of deadly little pots, sporting their bright labels. He paid no attention either to Cleo or the large dish of jam cooling on the bench.

'And dinner had better not be long, I've had a hell of a day,' he mumbled by way of a greeting as he disappeared into the lounge, turning on the television.

'Thanks for your interest in *my* day,' Cleo muttered bitterly under her breath while she cooked a pork chop and vegetables for his dinner. She'd lost her appetite and decided on cheese and crackers by herself in the kitchen.

'Whisky, now!' he shouted from the lounge. She silently prepared a strong whisky and soda and took it through to him.

When the food was cooked, Cleo served it attractively on a square white plate, liberally spreading the pork with the whole dish of jam left over from her afternoon's endeavours. She added a parsley sprig for garnish and stood back to check that it wouldn't attract criticism. She placed another large whisky and soda with the plate on a tray and carried the lot through to the lounge.

Cleo had only learned the bare facts about her consignment bound for the Piglet Café. She hadn't known about Elise's dad, Bill Dean, the dispatcher, or Mick the truck driver who both worked for the same company. Mick had pushed his semi-trailer along the road, careful not to exceed the speed limit. There weren't many points left on his licence. He looked at the time and made a quick calculation. He'd make it home in time to throw a couple of steaks on the barbie and enjoy a few beers with his wife and adult sons. In the trailer, he was carrying a mixed load of boxed dry goods bound for the depot. Nestled in among the boxes was one addressed to Piglet Café. Bill had okayed Mick's plan to unhook the trailer, leave it locked in the depot yard and bobtail home.

Mick was travelling on one of the few well-made sections of the highway, with a dual carriageway and a good width of breakdown lane on the left. He glanced in his rear-view mirror and frowned at the sedan coming up beside him. *Come on, idiot, you've got plenty of room, crank it up and get past me.* As the car drew level with his window, he glanced down into it. The lady in the front passenger seat was gesticulating wildly to the rear. The kid in the back seat was holding up a bit of paper that said ... *WHAT? Smoke?! Hell!* Mick waved a vague acknowledgement and quickly began slowing his truck, flicking on his hazard lights and pulling over into the breakdown lane as far off the road as he could.

As soon as he stopped, Mick jumped down from the cabin and began searching methodically along the right-side trailer tyres. Nothing. He went around the back and started searching up the left side. *There!* Second axle from the back. Smoke and the tiniest flicker of flames rising from the overheated bearing.

Mick raced back around the end of the truck and up to the cabin, scrambling in to grab the fire extinguisher. He pulled the safety pin on the extinguisher as he ran back to the quickly growing fire. He squeezed the handle on the extinguisher. Nothing.

'Bugger!' he swore, 'I *meant* to get that damned thing serviced.' He swung the useless red cylinder down and raced back towards the cabin.

His only hope now was to unhook the trailer and get the prime mover far enough away from the fire so it wouldn't burn too. Working quickly, Mick managed to unhook in record time and drove his truck up the road a safe distance from the savagely burning trailer. He turned and watched the all-consuming blaze. Deep within the fire, twenty-four small pots and one large catering-size jar of rhubarb, pear and garlic jam cracked and oozed their toxic contents into the unsalvageable mess.

Widow Lardner lay back in her softly scented bubble bath, idly pouring tiny bubbles from one hand to the other. A small smile played around her mouth. Death from complications of diarrhoea the coroner had said when examining Nathan's death, but she knew she had poisoned him. She still couldn't believe she'd left the toxic rhubarb leaves on the stems. Even less could she believe her good fortune when she learned that the truck carrying her consignment of poisoned pots to the Piglet Café had burned. *Some angel was watching over me*, she thought gratefully. *Not a very dignified death for Nathan*, she mused. *But he didn't give me much dignity in life.*

The bath was cooling again. Cleo's smile widened. Her business was growing beautifully. She was meticulously careful these days. Nothing was going to jeopardise what she had so carefully established. Cleo leaned forward, pulled out the plug and stood up, wrapping a large fluffy towel around herself.

CHAPTER 5

In the seedy downtown sector, Hadley Lardner parked his car in front of Tyche but didn't get out. He was deep in thought. Since his father's death, he had taken over running the tattoo parlours. There were three of them scattered across town. He had made a half-hearted attempt to check on the books, to get an idea of how profitable they were and make sure no one was ripping the business off. He decided there wasn't much to running a tattoo parlour. One had to maintain a stern presence, so no one took any liberties. Other than that, money seemed to just roll steadily in. He hadn't made more than a cursory inspection of the paperwork in the office at Tyche, feeling that there was no rush as long as the tattoo parlours kept ticking over.

He knew he was drifting. Since dropping out of university last year, Hadley had felt rootless. His father's death hadn't helped, although he hadn't been close to his father. He didn't know what he wanted, whether to go back to his studies, whether to change courses, or what. He realised he would need some kind of family income so his mother would remain comfortably off and not start asking questions. Like his father, he felt that the less she knew, the better. She had told him about Tyche but appeared to be ignorant of the extent of the business. Hadley dithered between wanting to keep the tattoo parlours and selling them and going into something different. He thought his mother was keeping busy developing her jam business. He'd rather she stayed focused on that. He was puzzled by her attitude towards his father's death. He felt she was being far more joyful, *yes, there was no other word for it*, she was far more joyful than you would expect a widow to be. *What really happened the night Dad died?* he wondered.

His father's death, although unexpected and sad, was in a way a godsend for Hadley. Dropping out of university had left him with a lot of knowledge but no qualifications and no income. He knew his brother Tobias made a comfortable living dealing cocaine and growing marijuana. The fool had been careless, got caught and ended up in court. Hadley would have to make sure that didn't happen again. He didn't mind how Tobias made his money, but he certainly didn't want him winding up in jail. Leaning back in the car, he watched the comings and goings in the street and idly considered going into business with Tobias. His pharmaceutical knowledge could be put to good use making other drugs and Tobias could use his contacts to expand sales. *Maybe we could open a gym selling body-building supplements and hide the drug sales among those sales. Of course, we'd have to find a quiet spot for the lab, a shed somewhere. Maybe Tobias could set up a greenhouse there as well and grow greater quantities of marijuana.* Hadley shrugged impatiently. *Tobias was too much of a cocky, immature idiot. Sure, he seemed to have a good income, but how long would it be before he dug himself back into trouble with the law?*

* * *

Walking out of his last lecture of the day into the late afternoon sunshine, Lex Lardner felt his mobile vibrate in his pocket. His face lit up as he saw it was Karah calling. 'Hi sweetheart, I'm just leaving uni now.'

'Oh Lex …'

He could hear the tears in her voice and his heart sank. He hated anything that made Karah unhappy. 'What is it, babe?'

'The drycleaner has ruined my beautiful cashmere top and now I've nothing to wear for our date!'

With an effort, Lex clamped his mouth shut on the relieved words, 'Is that all?' *Why couldn't she just wear another top if the drycleaner had ruined the cashmere top?* Karah in any top was beautiful to him. If she wore a hessian bag to the bar, it was far preferable to having to go to either of their parents' places or missing their date entirely. He sighed. 'Karah, babe, don't stress. If you don't want to go to the bar, we can just pick up a pizza and drive up to the lookout. It's a beautiful evening.

The city lights will look pretty.'

'It's not the same!' she wailed. 'I wanted to look beautiful for you.'

That was just who Karah was: a perfectionist, stubborn, persistent, clever, beautiful. He wished she could understand that he would love her if she was dressed in autumn leaves or anything else for that matter. Tall, slim, dark-haired. He adored the way her eyes flashed with anger or excitement or amusement. She was very animated and quick to respond whatever the situation. He couldn't believe how lucky he was to have her as his girlfriend.

'You always look beautiful to me! I'm looking forward to our evening. Please don't fret over your outfit, I want us to have a happy time together. We don't see each other often enough as it is. And you know I've got a late lecture tomorrow and you're going on that excursion on Thursday. What time are you due back from that?'

'It's a three-and-a-half-hour drive and I don't think the schedule allows us to leave there much before five or five-thirty. I think I'll be too tired to do anything after that. We're leaving at six in the morning!'

'Big day for you. Let's just go up to the lookout tonight. It'll be just us and it'll be relaxing.'

Karah Nester sniffed back her tears. She could see the sense of Lex's words because she was just as anxious to see him as he apparently was to see her. Oh, how she loved him!

'Oh Lex, as usual you make me see sense. I'm sorry, I shouldn't have made such a fuss. Sometimes things all get a bit much for me. But the top was almost brand new. Yes, let's have pizza at the lookout. Will you pick me up round seven?'

'Of course, I will! I can't wait.'

She made a kissing sound into the phone and ended the call. She looked at the ruins of her cashmere top being presented by the apologetic drycleaner. Although her family was very well off, she had opted to live independently from them while she completed her degree. It was a hard fight to get her parents to agree because they were very protective of her. Her waitressing job didn't cover too many luxuries after student accommodation, food and books. She had splurged on the beautiful soft cashmere a few weeks ago. She had loved wearing it and planned to wear it again tonight for her date with Lex. Not an expensive night out, just one drink, sipped to make it last while they snuggled on the shabby lounges in the basement bar downtown that gave gigs to bands just starting out. She and Lex didn't really listen to the music, just enjoyed the freedom to be with each other without their families present and without their timetables. Shrugging mentally, she resigned herself to the plan change, stiffened her shoulders and began to pay attention to the drycleaner's offer of compensation.

In his heart, Lex believed Karah was the love of his life. He simply adored her, but he worried about their future. He knew her family were very wealthy but he had heard unsavoury rumours about her father and how he made his money. He also knew from things Karah had said that both her parents were very watchful over her, particularly her father. She was quite vague about what her dad did.

Lex's brothers had hinted that there was something mysterious about their own father's death. He knew his father, Nathan, had been involved in some dubious activities. He guessed the family tattoo parlours wouldn't stand up to rigorous inspection. His brothers were supposed to be running them since his father's death, but Lex had a feeling his brothers had no idea what they were doing. *Would Karah's father have heard any rumours about my father?* He didn't think either of his brothers, Hadley or Tobias, would stand up as worthy people if given anything more than cursory investigation. They both seemed to be involved in some grubby dealings, Tobias especially. Lex wondered if Karah's father would disapprove of him, simply based on his own father's and brothers' reputations.

Lex felt very conflicted, knowing his love for Karah, realising how suspicious he was of Karah's family as well as suspecting there were some secrets hidden in his own family. *Why couldn't things be straightforward?* All he wanted was to be with Karah. *Couldn't her family just be happy for her that she was in a relationship that made her happy?* He realised he hadn't shared much detail with any of his family members about his relationship. *Why?* he mused.

*   *   *

Tobias Lardner had spent a hectic day. Parts of it had been very stressful, other parts had been ridiculous. He swigged beer and grinned again as he relived events.

Earlier, he had stood straight and uncomfortable in the austere courtroom. He had sat through a couple of intense interviews with his solicitor, a somewhat fussy man his brother had hired for him. To be honest, Tobias had the feeling Mr Dartmoor hadn't been overly impressed with him. The solicitor had given him many explicit instructions, too many for Tobias to remember even though he really did try to take it all in.

'Wear a suit, it makes a much better impression. Stand tall, it makes you look honest. Don't slouch, it gives the impression of guilt. Keep your face neutral. Smiling looks like you don't take this seriously.' That last instruction had made Tobias smirk. 'And for heaven's sake, don't smirk like that. Do you *want* to go to jail?'

Tobias felt nervous and overdressed in his suit. Those last words still rang in his ears as he waited anxiously for the decision to be made. He knew very well what faced him if he went to jail. When he had discussed his trouble with his brother, Hadley had spelled out very clearly just what was involved in being in jail. Tobias had no wish to go there. That didn't mean he was particularly remorseful over his crime. *What was wrong with growing a bit of weed? A man had to make a living, after all. But jail? No thanks, jail was a permanent record and a bad mark on one's character.* Quite clearly, Tobias was extremely unrepentant and somewhat deluded about the goodness of his character.

The judge's gavel came down with a crack, making Tobias jump.

'Mr Tobias Lardner, I find you guilty of cultivation and possession of cannabis in too great a quantity to qualify as "personal use". As this is your first offence, I will not give you a custodial sentence or record a conviction. Instead, I sentence you to one hundred hours of community service,' the grave voice intoned.

After a weighty pause, the judge continued, 'Be aware, that if you come to the attention of the police again, the consequences will be much more serious. Your hundred hours are to be served within the next eight weeks. You can choose to complete the hours in less time but if the hours are not completed within eight weeks, your case will come before me again with the possibility of more hours being added. You will discuss with your supervisor how your time will be rostered. The sentence is to be served under the supervision of Mr Steven Yackersley, head gardener at Lovely Banksia Nursing Home.'

Tobias was immediately overcome by an apparently violent coughing fit and buried his face in his hands. His shoulders shook with contained laughter and his sides ached. *Oh God, fancy sending me to do gardening! I can just plant my weed in the well-tended garden beds at Lovely Banksia!*

'Mr Lardner!' The judge's voice sobered Tobias and, tightly controlling his face, he looked towards the bench. 'Would you like a glass of water?'

Tobias replied in a voice still shaky with suppressed laughter, 'No thank you, Your Honour.'

'Dismissed!' The gavel banged down again; everyone stood, and the judge left with majestic strides.

With that problem settled, Tobias' mind quickly snapped to another. Reaching for his phone, he dialled his friend, Snake. Snake was known by that name to all his friends, although his loving mother had him baptised as Eric and would have been shocked to hear him referred to by any other name, especially Snake.

'Meet me at the cemetery. Got a job we need to discuss.'

Tobias only had a few minutes to wait in the peaceful lanes of the cemetery before Snake's white van coasted quietly to a halt behind him. He joined Snake in the van. They smoked a joint while Tobias outlined his problem. Imagining their minds were working brilliantly, they concocted the plan of kidnapping Elise.

Later, with Elise tied up in the back, Snake had driven his van eastward out of town. In a few short minutes, he was outside the built-up area, away from houses and streetlights.

He couldn't quite screw himself up to kill her just yet. Had to think about it and come up with a plan. He had no idea where the Hartseig Road that Tobias had mentioned was, but he had an idea where he could leave the girl for a while. Away to the west, rich grazing farms and horse studs spread, smooth green paddock after smooth green paddock edged with elegant, white-barked eucalypts; but where Snake was heading in the east were vast coal mines. Many of the farms on the east side of town had been bought by the coal companies for future expansion. To date, nothing had been done with these acres and most of the empty farmhouses and outbuildings still stood.

Snake drove fast and after forty-five minutes, the bitumen gave way to a gravel road which gradually deteriorated to a dusty track. Snake kept up the pace and Elise was thrown about with brutal force on the floor as the van slid and skidded around corners, banging over potholes. Several times her head hit the side of the van, leaving her stunned and semi-conscious.

Being away from crowded houses and suburban streets always made Snake edgy, especially at night. He was on his own because Tobias had remembered other business he needed to attend to. Snake imagined terrible things lurking just outside the reach of the headlights. Shadows came alive, leaping and changing, tree branches looked like arms reaching out at him. A kangaroo sprang across the road, making him swerve sharply and swear. He figured that the faster he went, the less time he would spend out of town. He was beginning to regret offering to get rid of the girl.

The swinging beams of the lights eventually showed Snake the dilapidated sun-bleached mailbox he was looking for. He slowed the van, turning left into a driveway, the sagging gate propped open with a stick. Down a short, curved track, overgrown with straggling grass, he pulled up in front of a weatherboard house. He switched off the engine but was too craven to turn off the lights. When he opened his door, the silence of the bush engulfed him like a blanket. The skin on his arms prickled and his eyes cut quickly from side to side. Adrenalin pushed his heart rate up and he felt defenceless and exposed. He was in a hurry to get back to town now. Quickly opening the back of the van, he grabbed Elise roughly, carrying her to the front door of the house. He flung open the door and froze. He couldn't see anything! *Geez, this is crap,* he hissed to himself. He stepped through the remembered doorway on his left, dumping the inert body unceremoniously on the floor, then spun on his heel and fled, slamming the outer timber door behind him. He ran to the van and locked himself in. He leaned back on the seat with a relieved gasp, feeling his heart pounding as if he'd just run a marathon. *Can't understand what people like about the country!* He shivered and turned the key. Revving the engine, he spun the van with a shower of gravel and raced back towards the security of well-known urban environs.

Snake broke all the speed limits driving back to town. Only when familiar streetlights cast their calming golden glow over the road and suburbia, did he begin to feel safer. He made his way downtown, parking the van in a No Parking zone outside a brightly lit pub. In the noisy comfort of the crowded bar, he quickly downed a couple of relaxing vodkas, then, feeling more settled, looked around for some buddies. He had a wide circle of friends and had no trouble finding a rowdy group to join. Soon he was well on the way to being as drunk as the rest of his mates and quickly put his trip to the country out of his mind.

When someone suggested moving to a less public venue for a little ganja or some crack, Snake willingly went along. A while later, the whole group were feeling mighty fine and ready for adventure. The nightlife in Sydney was calling, and Snake happily jumped into one of the cars driven by a more sober member of the group. Without a care in the world, they careered down the silver-lit freeway towards a city spree of mammoth proportions.

*   *   *

Dazed, Elise lay where Snake had dumped her. *Well, thank God, he hasn't killed me yet!* She felt hard timber on her hip, arm and cheek. Her head throbbed. Her mouth was dry, and her bladder was screaming for relief. Gradually her battered senses settled. *Have I been kidnapped? Where am I?* The silence told her nothing, the air felt dry and smelled slightly dusty. *I have to get this tape off my eyes. Oh, my phone! I'm lost without my phone!* As her thoughts rattled crazily, she felt sheer panic. She quickly realised that sensible thought was what she needed and forced herself to calm down.

First things first, check for injuries and get my hands free. She straightened her legs and wriggled her toes. *Oh no! I've lost one of my beautiful shoes!* Flexed her ankles. *Nothing seems broken but my left ankle is stinging. Legs okay. Hips? Fine.* Her back was sore, but she reasoned that the rough ride had simply worsened the damage from wrenching it that morning. *Was it only this morning? What time is it? How long was I in that van? Oh, my head hurts. Couldn't they at least have sat me in a seat?*

Still lying on her side, Elise arched her back, stretched her arms down and wriggled her hands around over her bottom. It was a squeeze and the cable ties bit into her wrists, but desperation forced her on. *Ahh, halfway there!* She drew her legs up and, one by one, pulled them through the loop her hands made, bringing her arms in front instead of behind her. *Free!* She quickly brought her hands to her face and ripped the tape from her eyes and mouth. *Ouch! There go a few eyebrows.* She was stunned to realise she could see nothing; it was pitch dark. *Okay, keep calm. You can still FEEL.* She reached down and took off her one remaining shoe. She rubbed her stinging ankle and realised it was cut and had been bleeding. Then, holding her shoe in one hand, she stood up. Groping slowly, her tied hands out in front of her, she took tentative steps forward until she reached a wall. *So I am in a house, or at least some sort of building.* She moved left, feeling the smooth gyprock, hoping to find a doorway. Instead, she found a corner.

Gradually she moved along and after a second corner and a few more slow sidling steps, she found an open doorway. *Where to now? Just keep going, I guess. This must be a house. Need to find a toilet.* Elise stumbled with her hands outstretched. *Eek, what's that?* She jumped back as her hands brushed against some curtains. *Get a grip,* she told herself sternly. *You can do this. Oh! It's so dark because the curtains are all closed.* She pulled the curtain aside and peered out. *No moonlight!* All she could see was the faintly starlit sky. *So, I'm not in town.*

After what seemed ages, groping along walls and through doors, Elise felt benches, shelves, a stove (*Ha! The kitchen!*), light switches (*No electricity connected*) and eventually identified a hallway. She crept along, guessing she would either arrive at an exit door or maybe bedrooms and a bathroom.

Success! She located the bathroom and dealt with the most pressing need, not the easiest of tasks with hands tied. *Relief!*

Now, how to get these ties off! Then I guess, keep exploring. She tucked her one blue shoe heel in the waistband of her jeans. *Why am I holding onto this shoe? My last link with home?* With both hands empty, she found the handbasin and tried the tap. *Water!* She cupped her hands under the flow and drank greedily. *Oops, hope it's clean. Oh well, too late now. But it tasted okay.*

Elise groped her way back to the kitchen, only taking a few wrong turns on the way. She was surprised how quickly she grew accustomed to being unable to see. She tried all the drawers in the kitchen, trying to find a knife or pair of scissors. There was nothing useful in the drawers. The handles on the drawers had extended sections outside the screws that fixed them to the drawers. She straightened her arms down and hooked the cable ties over the extension, then suddenly dropped her weight down. She didn't weigh much, and it wasn't enough to snap the ties. They just bit painfully into her wrists. *Bugger! What now? Sleep, I suppose, can't do much else in the dark.*

For no other reason than that was where she started, she groped her way back to the room she'd been dumped in and lay down. It was not comfortable on the bare timber floor, but for Elise, it had been a huge day and much to her surprise, she quickly fell asleep.

CHAPTER 6

'Morning, Ben. Seems we have a bit to do today. Glad to see you made an early start!'

Ben gave Kaylee a mock salute. 'Beat you by a good half hour, boss!'

Kaylee shrugged in surrender. 'Yeah, you got me there. Was interesting what Diego shared with us last night. Pity he didn't have much that was any help to us. Downtown sounds as seedy as ever. Evidently, by the sound of it, there is still plenty of policing for us to do in this town. How come he mentioned Tyche? Do you know anything about it?'

Kaylee rested her coffee cup on Ben's desk, careful not to disturb what she recognised as 'organised chaos' among the papers spread out.

'Apparently it came up in his investigations. There are three tattoo parlours with the name, in various parts of town, owned by the same bloke. The biggest one is downtown where the nightlife goes on. Good location, really, people get a bit of courage after a few drinks, head into the parlour, come out with some ink they may or may not later regret. I can't recall hearing of any trouble relating to Tyche specifically, but I seem to remember the owner died not long ago. Wonder who has it now? Diego wasn't too impressed with what he'd heard. He's only investigating them for the guy who owns the bookstore.'

'We'll have to look at all that more closely, but I think we'd better find Elise first. She's our priority. You go over to her office and see if you can access her laptop. Diego should help you. I was relieved he was so cooperative last night. Must be down to your macho-man charm.' She grinned at Ben, dropping her business-like tone.

'That's us, all boys together!' he responded cheekily, adding seriously, 'I'll give you a buzz round lunchtime, see where you are, and compare notes. What are you doing?'

Kaylee sighed. 'I guess I'm doing the horrible bit: talking to Elise's family.'

'Yeah, that's not nice.'

'Okay, good luck.'

She took her coffee and carried on towards her desk to check whether anything had come up during the night needing her attention. *How are we going to find a white van without anything to identify it?* she wondered. *Where could they have taken that poor woman, and why?*

Kaylee drove to the address she had been given for the trucking company where Elise's parents, Bill and Sharon Dean, worked.

Bill Dean put protective arms around Sharon's shoulders

as she sagged into him.

'Oh no!'

'Our little girl! Who would do that?'

'That's why I'm here, Mr and Mrs Dean, to see if you can tell us anything that might help us find Elise,' Kaylee said gently.

'I always had a bad feeling about this investigatin' business,' Bill rumbled unhappily.

Bill had been a dispatcher for Desmond Transport Company for years. From time to time, he had done some driving for them but these days, he preferred the comfort of the office to the rigours of the road. Sharon had continued to do the bookwork and wages for the company on and off over the years, when the demands of being a mum to three children had allowed. Since Elise had finished university, Sharon had worked full-time in the office of Desmond Transport. She and Bill enjoyed being able to travel to and from work together. Right now, it was very convenient for Kaylee to have them together and it was certainly a comfort for them to be with each other.

'When did you last speak to Elise? Was she worried about anything? Discuss anything from work?'

'She came over to us last weekend. We all had dinner on Saturday night for little Lily's birthday.'

'Lily is our granddaughter, Elise's niece.' Bill spoke with loving pride.

'Elise was fine. Happy. She played with the kids, had a few

drinks, just seemed normal.'

'Did she talk about work at all?' Kaylee delved gently.

'Just said she and Diego were busy as usual.' Bill looked at Sharon for confirmation. She nodded.

'She didn't say much other than that. She doesn't talk about work very often, said early on that she had to be careful about confidentiality.'

'I understand,' Kaylee nodded. 'Have either of you had any unusual phone calls yesterday or this morning?'

'Nothing.' Again, Bill looked at Sharon for confirmation and again she moved her head, tears welling in her eyes.

'What do we do?'

'There's not much you can do. We're working very hard to locate Elise. If you hear anything, either from her or from anybody else, please let me know immediately.' Kaylee passed Sharon her card. 'I promise we'll keep you up-to-date with any new developments. Finding Elise is our top priority but we might wait a while before making any public calls for assistance if you don't mind.'

Bill nodded. 'Whatever you think best. Can we tell the family?'

'Oh, for sure. You need them around you for support just now. Elise may have talked to another family member about something she didn't talk to you about. If they mention anything to you, let us know. It might be helpful. I know it's usual in situations like this to call for help from the public.

Diego has asked us not to follow that procedure. He says publicising Elise's identity will compromise her effectiveness in doing her job in the future. How do you two feel about that?'

Bill spoke hesitantly. 'I guess Diego knows best.'

'Well, how's this? We do as Diego asked for a few days and then review the decision in consultation with you and Diego.'

'Yeah, that's probably best.'

'In the meantime, you two just look after each other and try to always have one of your phones free in case of a call. There's no need to let us know where you are but I'm not sure either of you feels much like working. Could the company spare you for the rest of the day? You might be more comfortable at home.'

Bill nodded and stood up. 'I'll go see the boss now. I'll explain to him and ask him to keep it quiet. He's pretty good and I reckon I agree with you, Sharon should be at home.' He gave Sharon's shoulder a gentle squeeze. 'Wait here, love. I won't be long.'

Kaylee was relieved to have the unpleasant task finished. She hated the part of her job where she was responsible for delivering bad news, but she could see Bill and Sharon were going to be a loving support for each other. She hoped the horrible suspense of not knowing their daughter's whereabouts would not last long.

❋ ❋ ❋

In a second-storey flat across town, two brothers faced each other, one furious, the other defensive.

'YOU DID BLOODY WHAT?' Hadley yelled at Tobias. A vein stood out in his forehead, and he lunged for his brother. Tobias stepped nimbly backwards, eyes wide. He'd never seen his brother lose it like this.

'Hey, hey, cool it.' He spoke weakly, trying to calm his brother.

'COOL IT? COOL IT?' Hadley thundered. 'You stupid, idiotic moron! You expect me to cool it when you stand there and tell me you kidnapped a bloody private investigator? What the hell did you do that for? You didn't think it might be a good idea to discuss the investigation with me?'

'Did you *know* we were being investigated?' Tobias felt sudden resentment that his brother hadn't shared that information with him.

'Yeah, she cornered me the other day.' Hadley spoke dismissively.

'Ha! And you didn't think to share that with me? Thanks for nothing, brother.'

'I didn't tell her anything, but I figured she'd be back.' Hadley's hands clenched and unclenched at his side. He was trying very hard not to punch his brother's face. Tobias backed up a few more steps but Hadley advanced, towering over his brother. His face was twisted and red with rage. Violently he turned away and threw himself down on the lounge.

'You'd better come up with a bloody good explanation about this, Tobias, or I swear I will damned well kill you.' Hadley spoke slowly and clearly, his shoulders shaking with the effort of trying to calm down and regain some control over his fury. 'Jeez, I just dug you out of a mess yesterday! You're on a good behaviour bond, for God's sake!'

'I was tellin' Snake about that investigator ...'

Hadley leapt up. 'God! Don't you know anything, you completely witless fool? Our business is *our* business and only our business! You don't bloody share ANY of our business with anyone! Certainly not anything about us being investigated.' He massaged the back of his neck with hard angry fingers, pacing back and forth. 'Carry on,' he rasped. He knew Snake was Tobias' best friend, but he was not sure whether Tobias knew Snake worked for Damien Nester, the son of the man who had hired Elise to look into the Lardner family. Of course, Hadley didn't know for sure that it was the Nester patriarch who had ordered his family to be investigated but he guessed it was. His father had once hinted that there was no love lost between the two families but had not expanded on the information. Hadley also guessed the investigation had been ordered because his younger brother, Lex, was dating the treasured daughter of the family. Hadley was not sure of the depth of loyalty Snake had for his employer, whether he was to be trusted not to carry tales back to the Nester family.

'Well, sorry. But Snake and I go way back. Anyway, we were just tossin' ideas round to come up with an idea how to stop that woman investigatin' us.'

'Just because you and Snake "go way back" doesn't mean he's a smart choice to come up with any ideas. Don't forget, I've known him for just as long as you. I consider him to be unintelligent and unreliable, absolutely flaky, to be honest.' Hadley paused. 'So, the brilliantly intelligent Snake said, "Let's kidnap her", did he? Or were you the clever one to come up with the idea?' he snarled sarcastically.

'Okay!' Tobias snapped, abruptly tiring of his brother's attitude. 'So maybe it wasn't such a good idea. But it's done now.'

'And you want me to sort out another mess of your making, do you?' Hadley was still furious. 'I should just bloody tell the cops!'

'Christ, you wouldn't!' Tobias sat down, suddenly pale. He was beginning to realise that what had seemed like a clever idea was far from it and could have terrible consequences.

'Where is she?' demanded Hadley. 'No point wasting more time going over your stupidity.' He wanted to start sorting this out.

'If you'd trusted me a bit, we wouldn't be in this mess.'

'Oh, so suddenly *we* are in this mess, are we? I can just walk away you know, you damned fool. So, answer my question. Where is she?'

'I don't know.'

'YOU DON'T KNOW?' Hadley's forced calm instantly evaporated.

A few moments of silence passed while Hadley took deep measured breaths, trying to marshal some rational thoughts, instead of imagining his hands choking the life out of his brother.

'Okay. So how is it that you can be involved in a kidnapping and not know the whereabouts of the victim?'

'We had her in Snake's van. He was driving way too fast. I had to tell him to slow down, or the cops would've had us straight away.'

'Your first sensible action so far,' his brother growled sardonically.

'Yeah, well. Then I realised I was late meeting this dude at Tyche, not downtown, the one over in Bergen Circle. Snake said he could drop me off there and he'd deal with the girl. We were sharing a joint before he dropped me off, but the girl started kicking the side of the van, making a racket. Snake wanted to get going, so he left before I asked him what he was doing with her.'

'Really, your stupidity is stunning! So, you thought your plan all the way through to kidnapping her and no further. You don't know where she is. He'd "deal" with her. Does that mean hide her somewhere or kill her? You don't know if she's alive or dead. You've made no plan for a ransom. You have no thought as to how this situation will end.'

Tobias nodded unhappily.

'And you thought I'd be delighted with your brilliant idea! Did you and Snake organise feeding her, if she's alive? Has she got water? Or do you just hope she'll die? Did you check if she had her phone on her?'

Tobias slumped on a chair.

'Okay, okay. I'm sorry. But like I said, it's done now. I don't know where she is, alive or dead. I don't know if she's got food or water. I don't know if she's got her phone. I know it's a mess and now can you please help me sort it out?'

'Get in touch with Snake,' Hadley said roughly. 'If he hasn't killed her, she's gotta be kept alive while we sort out some plan. I don't want a murder on my head, or yours, you bloody useless idiot. Ring Snake.'

Hadley paced, frowning fiercely, while Tobias made the call. After a few moments, he hung up in disgust.

'He's not answering.'

'Oh, that's great, just great!' After a few moments' thought, Hadley snapped, 'Ring Feral. Maybe he knows where Snake is.'

Feral was Snake's older brother. The names their parents had given them were Patrick and Eric Carlton. Their lifestyle, habits and friends had made sure they were given their entirely appropriate nicknames. Only their parents and people in positions of authority used any name other than Feral and Snake.

'He doesn't know where Snake is either. Been trying to call him all morning. He'll let me know when he hears from him.'

* * *

Elise woke to the songs of butcherbirds and magpies. Her whole body ached. After the rough ride she'd had yesterday evening, sleeping on a cold hard floor was not the best treatment. Her most pressing need was the bathroom again and water for her thirst. *I'm hungry too,* she thought, sadly remembering last night's prawn salad. That seemed forever ago. *After that, I'm getting rid of these damned cable ties.* Her shoulders were stiff, and she longed to swing her arms freely. *Oh dear, then what? I've no idea where I am. Lucky it's summer. I'm hardly dressed for cold weather.*

In the early morning light, Elise discovered she was in an old farmhouse. *If I'd kept exploring, I'd have found this bed frame to sleep on!* Most of the drab-coloured curtains remained and were drawn across the windows. The only other furniture besides the bed frame was an old wooden chair. She looked more thoroughly for a sharp object to cut the cable ties off her wrists but found nothing suitable. In the kitchen, she found a closed door she'd missed last night. It led into a laundry with a concrete wash trough and finally, a door that led outside. She stood looking out, seeing a couple of dilapidated farm sheds, an overgrown garden and something that made her mouth water: a fig tree! She stepped out, feeling the rough weeds under her bare feet. *Maybe there are other fruit trees.* Under the fig tree, she reached up, selecting a large fig. *Delicious!* Unfortunately, the currawongs seemed to have found the tree as well and most of the fruit had been pecked off, leaving only stumps. Elise searched and found two more figs which she ate with gusto. The ties on her wrists were becoming very frustrating. *Got to get rid of these things.*

Then her mind registered something she'd seen by the back door but not paid attention to: an old-fashioned boot scraper with serrated metal edges. Many old farmhouses had similar tools by their back door, although these days, most workers simply left their boots outside. Leaving the fig tree, she returned to the back door. She knelt beside the scraper, placed her hands on either side of the rough metal and sawed carefully. Even taking care, she nicked her wrists several times before the hard plastic ties finally parted. *Phew, that's better! While I'm kneeling, better check my ankle.* There was a split across the bone that had bled freely but had now scabbed over. It was sore and bruised, and Elise figured the impact with the metal floor of the van must have caused the injury when she was thrown in.

Swinging her arms to ease the stiffness, Elise wandered around the overgrown garden. She saw onion plants gone to seed. A straggling tomato plant yielded a handful of cherry tomatoes. She found green carrot tops and pulled one up, taking it back to the kitchen to wash. It was old and stringy but better than nothing. Elise began to realise that without shoes, her soft feet would not take her far. She also recognised that she had better be careful with the available food. She had no idea where she was, or whether anyone would come for her. *What if that man from last night comes back? Should I hide if he comes back? Fight? Plead?* She vaguely recalled he'd picked her up easily to carry her inside so she would be no match in a fight. She went back out to the garden and sat in the sun trying to come up with a sensible plan. There were so many unknowns, it was a daunting task.

Come on, you're an investigator. So, investigate! Decisively, Elise stood up. She walked through the house and out the front door. She looked around for vehicle tracks. It seemed that only one vehicle had used the driveway recently and it had sprayed gravel when it left. She followed the overgrown drive up the slope to the dilapidated gate, eyes carefully fixed on the track. At the gateway, she saw that the vehicle (*the van?*) had come along the road from her right and gone back the same way. Looking left, she could see no fresh tracks at all. *Okay, so nobody comes out here much and to my right is the way back to town. How far? What if the guy comes back? I don't want to be here if he does. How far can I walk without shoes?*

Elise decided she would not be there if the man came back

but she needed to make some preparations before she left the farm. She walked back down the slope, through the house and began to explore the sheds.

* * *

Later that day in the police station, Kaylee reached for her ringing phone.

'Hey, Ben. What have you found out?'

'Where are you? We could grab some lunch and exchange info. I'm outside Marcus Street Shopping Centre.'

'Good idea. Grab me a chicken salad wrap and I'll see you at those seats in the atrium. Don't worry about getting me a drink, I've got water.'

'Right. You owe me, you know. You're making a habit of me buying and you not paying.'

Kaylee made a rude noise into the phone, then laughing, she disconnected, leaving Ben ruefully grinning and shaking his head.

Seated opposite each other in the busy atrium, the detectives settled into lunch.

'What did you find out from Elise's laptop?' Kaylee spoke through a mouthful.

'Look at you chow down! Must have had a hard morning,' Ben teased.

'You're forgetting, I was talking to her family.'

'Oh, yeah, sorry.' He held up a pacifying hand in response to her frown and changed the subject. 'You ready for this?'

Kaylee nodded.

Ben explained the Nestor-Lardner businesses and connections, detailing Lex and Karah's budding romantic relationship and Evander Nester's opposition to it.

'We need to sharpen up our act and get some official attention on both these families,' he added.

'This doesn't immediately progress our search for Elise. Poor woman. But it does show a connection between the two families, and we know for sure that Elise was checking out the Lardners. How about you go back to the station and get some help to interview everyone in the Nester and Lardner families. See if they can all be questioned at about the same time to eliminate the possibility of them concocting stories.'

'Right, boss.'

'Oh, by the way,' Kaylee added as an afterthought. 'Did you hear about a serious car accident down the freeway close to Sydney last night?'

'No. Anything significant for us there?'

'Among the victims were a group of locals. One of them is on life support in North Sydney, two others are critical, the rest have minor injuries. Apparently, they'd all been drinking, smoking, using cocaine and were speeding and acting the fool. Real recipe for coming to grief. Of course, it ended in disaster and unfortunately, a commuter heading home late was involved in the smash. He's one of the critical ones.'

'A mess. Are you following that up? Need to make sure the local families of victims are informed if they don't already know, social media being faster than the bush telegraph these days.'

'Yeah, I'm on it. Thanks, Ben. As usual, if there's bad news to be broken, I get the job.'

'Comes with the territory, boss,' he quipped, trying to cheer her.

'Ha! I guess so. I'll be in touch later. Thanks for lunch,' she added with a cheeky laugh.

Ben scowled, grinned and waved as he walked away.

CHAPTER 7

Various machines could be heard hissing and giving muted beeps beside the bed of a male patient in the dimly lit Intensive Care Unit of St Giles Hospital in North Sydney. A mechanical ventilator rhythmically pumped air into his lungs as he lay unconscious on the bed. Calmly, a nurse in blue scrubs examined the readings on the computer screen, checking for abnormalities in the readings. *This poor lad is in a bad way, and we still don't know who he is.* She straightened the sheet across his chest, then stood for a moment studying what she could see of the pale face. The victim suffered severe injuries during the accident. He had undergone emergency surgery and would need more. Medication was keeping him deeply sedated but alive. It was not yet known whether his brain would swell further because of the shaking it had received when the car rolled down the embankment. As she looked down at the patient, pondering his identity, she heard soft footfalls behind her. Turning, she quietly greeted the doctor. 'Any ID for this poor lad, yet?'

'Yes. He's Eric Carlton, from Muswellbrook.'

'Can we contact a next of kin?'

'One of the other people in the car has given us the phone number of a brother, name of Patrick Carlton.'

* * *

Fishing his ringing phone out of his pocket, Feral grunted a mumbled greeting.

'Is this Patrick Carlton?'

Feral snapped to attention. Few people called him Patrick, usually only his mother or someone in authority.

'Speaking.'

'This is Doctor Alex Milford-Wreath from St Giles Hospital in North Sydney. Is Eric Carlton your brother?'

'Yes.' Feral realised he was holding his breath.

'Eric has been in an accident and is in intensive care. Who is his next of kin?'

'Um, I don't think he's nominated anyone. Would that be our parents?'

'Yes, probably. Give me a phone number for one of them, please.' As with many of his colleagues, the doctor was forever pressed for time, and he spoke briskly.

'What happened? What's wrong with him?'

'How about you give me the contact details of your parents. I'll tell them, and you can go to them for details. They'll probably need you to give them support and help make arrangements ...'

'Funeral arrangements?' Feral heard the panic in his voice as he interrupted the doctor.

'No. We need to talk to them about his condition. He's in Sydney and I gather you're in Muswellbrook. They'd probably like to be with him.'

'Oh, right.' Relieved, Feral relayed his mother's details to the doctor.

No sooner had he disconnected from that call, than his phone rang again.

'Feral! Did you get in touch with Snake? I need him urgently.' Tobias spoke rapidly.

'Can't help. He's had an accident in Sydney.'

'In Sydney? When did he go to Sydney?'

'I dunno. When did you see him last?'

'Yesterday, late. What was he doing in Sydney?' A million different scenarios splintered through Tobias' brain. *Did Snake take the girl to Sydney?*

'Your guess is as good as mine. I gotta go, mate. Gotta drive the parents to the hospital. The doctor said to come.'

'Oh hell, that's bad. Sorry to hear it, mate.' Since Feral didn't know what Snake had been up to with Tobias, he had no way of knowing how very bad the situation was, both for his brother and for Tobias, and not least, for Elise.

Tobias quickly called Hadley and relayed the disastrous news, holding the phone away from his ear in anticipation of the explosion.

*   *   *

In the police station, Ben had gathered a group together and was explaining to them who he wanted questioned, why and how he wanted it to be done. He had reached the detail of Elise being bundled into a white van when a hand shot up.

'What is it, Jason?'

'I was downtown this morning and one of the publicans waved me down to show me a white van parked in a No Parking zone. Would have been legal last night but of course not during business hours. I wrote a ticket and stuck it under the windscreen wiper.'

Ben felt a fizz of excitement. He knew there were many white vans on the road but this one could be the one Mavis saw Elise being shoved into, and could possibly be a valuable lead.

'Well done, Jason. We need to take a closer look at that van. Get the rego off the duplicate of the ticket and get in touch with the owner right now, please. If, and it's a big IF, it is the van Elise was taken in, it could give us lots of answers.

*   *   *

Bill and Sharon anxiously went over and over the horrible news of their daughter's apparent kidnapping. Bill rang his daughter, Rebecca. She immediately offered to come round and be with them but Bill, aware of her busy life with three children, declined the offer, saying he'd call if he heard anything. He asked her to let her brother, Brad, know as well. Sharon rang her brother Burt's number. He had a cattle and produce farm west of town, near Wheeler, which he ran with his lively wife, Gisella. Sharon loved Gisella for her warm and generous nature. She knew Gisella would be very sympathetic but still upbeat about a happy outcome. She felt that just now she needed a strong 'dose of Gisella'.

'Oh Sharon! Caro, what terrible news. How you coping? What can we do? Burt will be so sorry. Why we hear nothing on news?'

'Because she's a private investigator ... her partner, you remember Diego? He thinks telling everyone who she is might make it hard for her to work in future.'

'Oh, yes, makes sense. Can't come in and see you because we flat out with Burt's arm in plaster. Not enough hours in a day. We dragging Silvio away from his work all the time to help us. Is not all bad though,' she giggled happily. 'He bring baby Oliver when he come to help and I get to mind bambino. He so cute! Come out, visit on the weekend. Do you good. Police helping you?'

When she was excited or worried, Gisella tended to forget all her carefully learned English. Sharon smiled at Gisella's disjointed conversation.

'Maybe we will come out on the weekend, Gisella. It would be nice. I'll let you know.'

They talked for a few moments more and then Sharon ended the call.

'Bill, maybe we could go out to Burt and Gisella's on the weekend if we've had no word. It'd be nice to get away from the house instead of sitting here worrying and waiting.'

*　*　*

Meanwhile, Elise was drawing on both her imagination and her practical nature. In one of the farm sheds, she found an abandoned cast-iron stew pot. She also discovered a quantity of twine hanging from a wall hook. The twine had been used on hay bales and was in loops about two metres long. She carried these finds back to the house via the vegetable garden where she foraged all the edible fruit and vegetables she could find, carrying them in the pot. She reasoned that if she was really hungry, even a raw potato would be palatable. She dumped her haul in the kitchen and returned to the shed. Not finding what she sought there, she tried a second, more dilapidated shed. *Aha!* A heap of abandoned beer bottles covered in dust, straw and spiderwebs caught her eye. She selected two and carried them to the back door. Crouching beside the step, she carefully funnelled handfuls of fine dust into each bottle.

Elise knew that when there was no hot water or detergent available, fine dust or sand and water could be vigorously shaken to act as a scour to clean bottles. She very thoroughly carried out the process twice on each bottle, hoping that would be sufficient to clean out any dangerous residue. The bottles were to carry her drinking water. She washed all the root vegetables, potatoes, carrots and parsnips and laid them on the bench to dry. She screwed up her nose, surveying what was to be her food for the foreseeable future. *Oh well. Weight loss here I come!* Her search of the garden had added some lemons and a few small apples. She had seen rhubarb but remembered reading somewhere that it could be toxic, so she left it in the garden. A couple of handfuls of mixed raspberries, strawberries and what looked like blackberries completed her haul. She knew the soft berries would not last long and decided to eat them first.

Leaving her clean bottles and vegetables to drip dry, Elise headed deeper into the house. She carefully took down a large drab curtain. *This will be my cape for warmth at night as well as camouflage if I must hide from Van Man.*

Next, she selected the two sturdiest curtains. She took them outside and using the rough saw on the boot scraper, ripped and cut them into four smaller squares. Her aim was to sandwich soft grass between two layers of curtain then gather the lot around her foot and fasten it in place with twine, repeating the process with the other two squares to make a pair of primitive shoes. She hoped this makeshift footwear would help protect her feet for however long she had to walk. She figured she could replace the squashed grass each day.

She chose a curtain to hold her food, intending to use twine to fasten it to a stout stick to carry over her shoulder. Her final task was to rip some curtains into strips. She would tie a loop around the neck of each bottle, drape the strip around the back of her neck and carry the bottles dangling in front of her. *Can I really do this?* She rested her head tiredly in her hands. Abruptly, she decided not to give up. She was leaving.

She took the old stew pot out the front of the house and half-filled it with gravel from the driveway. She would have preferred to fill it, but she knew that would make it too heavy for her to lift. Lugging it to the front door, she shoved it inside. Elise scratched around under a tree and found a slim stick which she broke in half. She wedged the sticks under the door, one from each side, effectively jamming the door about a hand span open. The door would require a strong shove to get it open, but the sticks ensured it would stay in place and not blow open or shut in the wind. She located the old chair she'd seen earlier and using it as a ladder, she hefted the stew pot. She carefully balanced it on top of the door, leaning it slightly against the wall for stability. Climbing off the chair she dusted her hands on her pants and grinned, visualising Van Man getting showered with gravel and perhaps a heavy cast-iron pot when he came through the door.

In the kitchen she packed her meagre supplies and filled the water bottles. She used the bathroom one last time, wondering how long before she would have that luxury again. Then she shrugged philosophically. *People did okay without toilets for thousands of years.*

She left the house by the back door, closed it firmly, and silently sent thanks to the farmers who had left her so much when they walked off their farm. She hoped fervently to find similar bounties along the road until she was rescued. Sitting under the fig tree, she picked grass and stuffed her 'shoes', tying each one securely with the twine. The lucky find of an old rake in the garden gave her a perfect stick to tie her food bundle to. Once her belongings were bestowed, she realised she would not be able to move with any speed especially with the lidless full water bottles dangling in front of her. She hoped she would only have to hurry off the road and hide if she heard Van Man coming. *I hope there are some bushes to hide in if he comes along!*

CHAPTER 8

The Nester household was currently not a happy home. Rhea was bored and angry. Evander, her husband, was surly and resentful. It had not always been like this. Their married life had begun happily enough. Children and a succession of golden retrievers had followed quickly. Rhea was a devoted mother. Evander ran a pawn shop and quietly fenced stolen goods, a fact he didn't share with his wife. Money was made and life was comfortable. There had been the usual ups and downs with childhood illnesses, pets ageing and dying, and academic and sporting awards. School years passed in a busy blur. Their eldest son Damien now ran a garage, and their second son Christos was employed there as a spray painter. Evander had 'negotiated' the cheap purchase of the garage as part of a debt-clearing deal, using veiled threats of violence. The garage, Golden Motors, dealt in the repair and maintenance of luxury vehicles.

Karah, their cherished daughter, was beautiful and bright. She could be quick to anger and quick to forgive, quick to see humour and quick to accept a challenge. Her greatest fault was that she could be infuriatingly stubborn. Her sunny nature made her popular both at school and at university where she was currently studying environmental science.

It was only after the children had grown up and embarked on building their own versions of cloud nine, that Rhea's happy dreams had turned into nightmares of loneliness and dissatisfaction. With both her sons well settled and Karah in high school, Rhea had found herself with time on her hands. She wanted other interests besides homemaking and mothering. She joined a small watercolour painting group, deciding that whether she had any talent or not, she would at least make new friends. They were a boisterous group, energetic, enthusiastic, happily sharing wine and cheese to help the sessions along. One day, the group leader, a friendly and easy-going woman in her fifties, suggested they should head downtown and try their hands at capturing the essence of the seedy area. Reconvening downtown, the five women filled most of the street, sitting on camp stools with their easels and paintboxes in front of them. Passers-by grinned indulgently as the women chattered eagerly about the scenery. It was colourful, even gaudy in spots, drab and ageing in others. Rhea's eye was caught by an old bent man standing in the candy-striped doorway of a tiny barbershop wedged in between a tattoo parlour and a grimy second-hand bookstore. She felt her imagination stir as she pictured the old man's life trimming hair and shaving clients over the years. She fancied she saw him watching the passers-by, some with fresh tattoos, some with old books, greeting those he knew. She felt he would have many tales to relate about the changing times in the street.

Quickly she sketched in the street scene, being careful with perspective. She drew in the tiny old man and made notes about the colours she saw. She wanted her finished painting to show the contrast between the mundane barber shop and the exotic tattoo parlour. Its sign was garish orange and green with the word Tyche in spiky black letters. It would be easy to make the bookstore look very dull next to the red barbershop stripes and the vivid tattoo shop sign.

Over the next few days, Rhea worked on her painting, pleased to see her visualisation of the contrasts in the street scene coming to life on the thick paper. She loved the way she had achieved the intensity of colour in the tattoo sign and the way it helped to really dull down the bookstore. The barber's poles added a cheerful touch to keep the painting alive.

Evander had paid only passing attention to Rhea's comments about her painting lessons. He still loved his wife but as happens in some marriages, he took her for granted, knowing she would be there with his dinner every evening, available for a shared drink while they discussed their day. They didn't share many interests now the children were becoming independent. He preferred to drop into the garage for a while after he closed his shop and exchange trade gossip with his sons.

When her painting was finished, Rhea was delighted to see she had achieved her aim. The group admired her work, agreeing that she had real talent. She propped the street scene on the coffee table in the living room to show Evander that evening.

Evander took one look at the painting and his face flushed angry red. 'What the bloody hell is this?'

Rhea was stunned. 'Th–th–the painting group I told you about. What's wrong?'

'Wrong? Wrong? You didn't tell me you were hanging round that tattoo parlour! What were you doing there?'

Rhea struggled to explain but everything she said was misinterpreted and Evander just grew more enraged. The evening was ruined, and Rhea silently took her painting and went to bed in mystified tears.

They didn't speak for days. Finally, Rhea couldn't stand it any longer. 'Evander, love, please explain to me why my painting upset you so much. I wasn't in the tattoo parlour. I never saw it before. I just used it as part of the scenery in my painting.'

Evander sighed heavily. 'I'm sorry. I overreacted.'

'But the place must mean something to you,' Rhea persisted.

'It's a long story.'

'I think I need to hear it. I didn't think we had any secrets.'

'This was before I met you. It's a family thing.'

Haltingly, Evander told Rhea a part of his family history she had no inkling of. Evander's grandfather, Georgios Nasse and his brother, Spiros, ran a lucrative SP bookmaking shop from which they also sold sly grog in Sydney in the 1920s. Close by their shop was a brothel owned by Alexis Ladas. Through sources unknown, Alexis had a constant supply of high-quality alcohol for his clients, which drew custom away from the Nasse sly grog shop. This worsened the enmity that already existed between the Nasse and Ladas families. The hostility between them was something they had brought to Australia from their home country, a long-standing vendetta the far-back origins of which neither family had a clue. They simply clung blindly to the ill-feeling as they had been indoctrinated by their embittered fathers.

In those long-ago days, Sydney had a prolific and very profitable illegal sector. In this sector, each participant jealously guarded their business, always with an eye open for anyone trying to muscle in. It was not a relaxing environment. Everyone was looking out for themselves, watching for the police and alert for trespassers and opportunists, not to mention gang violence. On most days, tensions were high and the mood volatile. Any deals that were contemplated had to be approached with great care and tact, because it was preferable to keep turf wars to a minimum to avoid police scrutiny.

One evening, the air was heavy with a brewing thunderstorm. People were hurrying to complete their business before the expected downpour. Spiros Nasse was working at the back of his store with an employee, trying to ensure it was as waterproof as possible. Hearing noises in the shop, he rushed in, surprising two masked thieves. He charged at the men, calling his employee to help him. The employee, peeping in from out the back, saw the scuffle and fled, never to be seen again. Defending his shop alone, Spiros was fatally stabbed during the attack.

Although the murderous raid was investigated by the police, no culprit was charged. Georgios, for no other reason than the vicious family vendetta, and the proximity of the Ladas brothel, blamed Alexis for the robbery and his brother's death. This implacable belief was passed on to following generations. Evander's father moved from the area and made a half-hearted attempt to make a new life away from the family feud by changing his surname to Nester. Even so, he strenuously indoctrinated Evander, as he had been by his father, that the Ladas family were bad to the bone and never to be trusted.

Alexis Ladas made a great deal of money from his brothel, eventually marrying one of his working girls. He gave her a lavish lifestyle, funded by importing alcohol for (legal) supply to Sydney's many hotels. Despite her comfortable lifestyle, his wife was not happy. She wanted all traces of her previous life wiped out and insisted Alexis change his surname from Ladas to Lardner.

When Evander and Rhea married and moved to

Muswellbrook, Evander noticed the tattoo parlour with the Greek name Tyche. Having an interest in the workings of the seedy downtown area and always keeping his finger on the pulse, he investigated who owned the place. Although the owner's name, Nathan Lardner, had no clear link to Ladas, Evander was very suspicious and kept a close eye on the business. Gradually, his suspicions hardened into certainty that Nathan Lardner was a descendant of the Ladas family. He resolved to keep his family well away from Tyche and the Lardner family.

During Evander's narrative, Rhea's eyes had shown her shock at the violent story she had not suspected was part of her much-loved husband's background.

'And so, Rhea,' Evander said heavily as he concluded the narrative, 'you have to stay away from there and anything to do with them.'

'I think it's ridiculous to be carrying on a feud you don't even know the origins of,' Rhea said strongly.

'Well, it's part of my family culture. I don't feel good about abandoning it and, besides, that Nathan Lardner was a low-life. I heard he sold drugs through that tattoo shop.'

'Yes, but you only *heard* that, you don't know for sure. What happened to innocent until proven guilty?'

'Look, Rhea, let's just drop it. If you've no reason to be near that area, fine. Go somewhere else for your art lessons or whatever.'

Rhea disliked having the law laid down in such a

high-handed way by her husband. 'Okay. Subject closed. Do I have to ask permission before I choose another activity?' She couldn't resist the sarcasm; her resentment was still too close to the surface. They settled into an uneasy truce. Rhea depended more and more on the ageing dog, Maizie, for comfort. She groomed the dog, walked her, played with her, spoiled her with treats and new collars.

When Maizie died, Rhea was devastated. She had lavished all her affection on the dog because Evander had become so withdrawn since sharing his family history. Closely following Maizie's death, Karah received her acceptance into university. She bluntly broke the news that she intended to fund her own studies. Both Evander and Rhea were stunned and hurt by her refusal to accept their offer of financial assistance. This pushed another wedge between husband and wife on top of the one that had developed when Evander revealed his family's feud with the Ladas family.

After airing the history Rhea had not suspected, it had taken some weeks for the unsettled air in the house to finally calm to impersonal friendliness, barely friendliness, really, more indifference. Rhea was still bored. She was deeply lonely without a canine companion. She decided it was time she took steps to change her life. Her first act was to buy herself a golden retriever pup. She called her Millie and jumped straight into enrolling her in obedience school, working with her, playing with her and generally being a mother to the dog now that her children no longer depended on her.

While playing in the park with Millie, Rhea noticed she quickly began to feel breathless trying to keep up with the boisterous pup. Rhea joined a gym. Although shy at first, she was relieved to notice many women round her age who seemed to be on the same journey as herself: children flown and gone, opportunities to concentrate more on themselves, chances to make new friends.

One such woman was dark-eyed Cleo Lardner.

CHAPTER 9

Feral was with his parents in their small, rented house in a quiet suburban street. His mother was crying. He felt like she had been crying since he arrived earlier. He understood she was upset but all these tears were becoming irritating. Crying women upset him and he was already very upset. He and Snake had a close relationship, being separated in age by barely a year and sharing many friends.

'Are we ready?' Feral had been trying to organise his parents for the trip to Sydney, to Snake, but they just seemed unable to get their act together and he was becoming frustrated. If he had been a psychologist, he would have realised a severe shock can immobilise the thought processes of normally sensible people.

Feral's parents were strong, down-to-earth people with a background in farming. He had seen them cope with the changing demands of a slowly advancing drought on the farm. He had seen them crack into immediate, effective action when faced with raging bushfires. He had seen them operating as a team, methodically moving stock and equipment to high ground in preparation for rain-filled creeks to flood. At those times, it seemed the understanding between them hardly required them to speak to each other. Now, these two practical people had been reduced to a state of shaking fogginess, unable to think, to plan, to act.

Feral hopped from foot to foot. He had arrived at the house shortly after the doctor had broken the news of Snake's condition. They were in pieces, his mother crying and his father murmuring incoherent words of solace. Feral told them to pack a bag each while he went to his place to pick up some clothes. He told them he'd drive them to the hospital, and he was anxious not to delay their departure. When he returned to their place, it seemed they hadn't moved. All he wanted to do was race to Snake's bedside. He was trying to get them to start packing when there was a knock on the door. *What now?* Turning from trying to push his mother towards her bedroom, he glimpsed a police car through the front window.

He yanked the door open. 'What do you …?'

Kaylee smoothly interrupted, holding up her ID. 'I'm looking for Mr and Mrs Carlton. And you are …?'

'Feral. Um. Patrick. Um, Patrick Carlton. I'm their son.'

Kaylee guessed from his rattled manner that the task of breaking bad news was done for her.

'Detective Sergeant Kaylee Bradshaw, Muswellbrook Police. Can I come in and speak to you all? It won't take long.' She stepped forward as she spoke and Feral automatically stood back for her.

'Mum, Dad!' he called. 'The police are here.'

He heard his mother's anguished cry and his father's rumbling attempt at comforting her. After a short while, they shuffled into the room. Kaylee gestured towards the lounge and Mr Carlton guided his wife gently towards it.

'Patrick, would you make your parents a strong sweet cup of tea please? It will help them calm down a bit. Have one yourself, you look like you could do with it.'

Could do with a snort of coke and a double scotch, more like. Better than tea. Feral shrugged and disappeared into the kitchen.

Mrs Carlton sobbed out loud. 'Is he …? Is my Eric …?'

'Now Mrs Carlton, you've just had some very bad news and I'm not here to tell you any worse. Eric is in hospital in Sydney. In Intensive Care. He's getting the best care. He's in an induced coma. How did you hear about his accident?' Kaylee spoke slowly, using her most soothing voice. She knew she had no chance of ever understanding the agonising torment these people were feeling just now. All she could hope to do was ease their pain a little by helping in any way she could.

'A doctor rang.' Mr Carlton spoke heavily. 'They're doing all they can. He said we should get there as soon as we could.'

'How will you get there? Is Patrick going to drive you? Do you need me to talk to any employers for you?' Kaylee didn't rush her questions.

'My wife and I are retired. Used to have a farm out east of town.' Mr Carlton spoke slowly. Kaylee was relieved to see her calm and measured questions were beginning to help him think clearly. She hoped their rural background had given them some experience in dealing with crises. Mrs Carlton's tears were becoming more of a wet sniffle than the wailing sobs they had been.

Patrick came in bringing two steaming mugs. Mrs Carlton reached out gratefully and cupped her hands around the soothing warmth. Mr Carlton put his cup on the coffee table looking as if he'd rather a stiff drink.

'I'm just helping them get a few things together and then we're off,' Patrick volunteered. 'They're not very familiar with Sydney.'

'Have you explained to your boss? I'm guessing you have a job.'

'I rang him when I heard. Snake, ah, sorry, Eric and I work at the same place.'

Some tiny instinct prodded Kaylee to ask one more question. 'And where's that, do you mind?'

'Golden Motors. My boss is Damien Nester.'

'Thank you, Patrick. I won't keep you any longer. Mr and Mrs Carlton, I understand your anxiety and I am very sorry for your troubles. If there's anything I can do to help you, please call me.' Kaylee pushed her card into Mrs Carlton's hand. She turned to Patrick. 'You've had a terrible shock. Make sure you drive safely to avoid adding to your problems.'

Feral nodded. Mr Carlton rested his hand on his wife's shoulder while she sipped her tea. 'We'll be right, thanks. Patrick will look after us.'

With relief, Patrick closed the door behind Kaylee. His parents seemed calmer now and he hoped they would soon be on their way.

*　*　*

Back at the police station, Kaylee walked into a hive of excited activity. 'What's all this?' She smiled at Ben.

'Nothing,' he replied straight-faced. 'This is our normal way of working.'

'Yeah, right. Well, I'll be at my desk if you need me.' Kaylee knew Ben well enough to ignore his hints because that immediately made him impatient to share any news.

'Wait till you hear this, boss.' He hurried after her to her desk. 'We've found the van they took the girl in!'

'Oh, great work! Fill me in, straight away please.'

He grinned. 'Jason put a ticket on a van outside a pub downtown. We traced the owner through the rego, but we can't contact him.'

Kaylee risked a wild guess. 'Let me see, would that be one Eric Carlton?'

She laughed out loud as Ben's face fell. 'How did you know?'

'You're not the only one who has been busy, you know. He and his brother work at Golden Motors owned by Damien Nester.'

'You *have* been busy!'

Quickly they stopped kidding around and excitedly shared their news. Kaylee explained about her conversation with the Carltons.

'He's in a coma?' questioned Ben.

'Yes, apparently in a bad way. His brother and parents are on their way to Sydney now.'

Ben's brow furrowed worriedly. 'Well, boss, we've been over that van. We got Clicks and Paul down there. They put police tape around it. There are blood stains in the back on the floor. The van is dusty like it's been in the country but hard to know how recently. I've asked Clicks and Paul to take samples off Elise's toothbrush, or anything else that might yield DNA, as a matter of urgency to see if we can match the bloodstains in the van with hers. What if he was acting alone and he's the only one who knows where Elise is?'

'Oh my goodness! What a terrible possibility. Maybe he put her in another vehicle and dropped her off somewhere on the way to Sydney before the accident. Did they check the accident site thoroughly? She might have still been in the car, thrown clear when it crashed. Jason ...' Kaylee beckoned the young police officer. 'Can you get in touch with the team investigating that crash on the freeway? Double check with them that there was no evidence of another passenger who may have been uninjured in the crash and ran away.'

She frowned at Ben. 'Oh dear, we really need to be working as quickly as we can. We simply can't let too much time pass before she's found. Was there a lot of blood? I wonder if she's badly hurt. What did questioning the Nester and Lardner families turn up?'

'They're a rough lot. Evander Nester bought Golden Motors during some times of trouble for the previous owners. It looks like he applied some heavy pressure to get them to sell to him and leave town. Since then, the two sons, Damien and Christos have been running the garage. Apparently, cars turn up unobtrusively on trucks from Sydney, are cleverly given new identities and are sold on, often interstate. Very lucrative. Evander has a pawn shop which also seems to earn more than it should, possibly fencing stolen goods. There's a sister, Karah, a university student. She's the one in a relationship with the Lardner boy, Lex. He's also a student. The Nester mother, Rhea, doesn't seem to know much about the family businesses, just enjoys a wealthy and idle lifestyle.'

'What about the Lardner family?'

'Same, basically. Oddly though, in these days of equality, both mothers seem not to know or care much about the family source of wealth.' Ben detailed his findings. He added, 'Cleo is not exactly grieving her late husband. He seems to have been a controlling bully.'

'Well done, you and your team. A very productive afternoon from you all. So where to from here?'

'I think the first thing we need to do is find out if Eric was using his own vehicle and hadn't loaned it to someone. Paul gathered prints off the steering wheel and driver's door handles. Same prints, and on the back door too. Need to see if we can match them with Eric's. Also, if he did it, was he acting alone?'

'The brother, Patrick, might know. He gives the impression they're close.'

'I'll ring him and double-check. You got his number, did you?'

'Yes, here you are.' Kaylee handed Ben her notebook. 'And nobody rang any alarm bells when the two families were being questioned?'

'Well, the vibe from Tobias and Hadley was described as "edgy and barely cooperative" and they revealed very little. I think we'd better do some follow-up on them both fairly quickly. Remember, Nester senior was having the Lardner family investigated and now the investigator has been taken. It's too much of a coincidence not to be connected in my opinion.'

Kaylee had too much respect for Ben's hunches to discount his words. 'Right. Didn't you say you had an appointment later today?'

Ben glanced at his phone. 'Oh heck! Yes. Gotta go, or I'll be late.'

'Okay. First thing tomorrow, you and I pay Hadley and Tobias a visit.'

'Right-o, boss. See you then.' Ben waved briefly as he grabbed his keys.

* * *

Hadley and Tobias were at Tyche downtown in a back room. Hadley sat in the reclining office chair, with Tobias opposite, less comfortably occupying a side chair. Smoke filled the air with the characteristic ganja smell, but the weed hadn't yet eased the tension that hung around the brothers like a cloak. Each had a shot glass in front of them and there was an open bottle of bourbon on the desk between them. Tobias tried to lighten the mood.

'You know, bro, I never told you about my last year at high school, how Snake got his nickname. You'd moved out of home, remember? You were trying your hand at independent living.'

'What do you mean *trying*? I seem to remember my scrawny brother constantly having a go at edging his way into my pretty successful party life.'

'Yeah, yeah. Anyway, back to my story. Ah, well, no point telling you I wasn't really into the dismal school scene. Neither was Snake. We still called him Eric at that stage. We were wagging one day, bored. But had to stay outta sight of, you know, Dad and anyone from school. We went down the back of the lake, hard for anyone to see us there. Just mooching along, skimming stones and throwing them at the ducks.'

'Riveting story so far,' Hadley interrupted sarcastically.

'Shut up. I'm building up to it.' Hadley refilled their glasses and Tobias passed him the joint.

'Anyway, Snake nearly steps on this snake. Frightened the life out of me but he was pretty cool about it. Quick as lightning, he bends down and grabs the thing just behind the head. The rest of it was lashing about and wrapping itself around his arm. He never turned a hair. He shoved the thing in my face! Its bloody mouth was wide open. I could see drips of venom on its fangs. Scared me rigid! But he was just laughing. Bastard.'

'What'd he do with it?'

'Took off his backpack, slipped the snake inside and zipped it shut. Then he put his backpack back on! No way I could have had that thing on my back with a snake in it! Then he said we should go back to school. I ask you. Why did he want to go back to school? We were having fun wagging. Anyway, back we went. The lunch bell had gone and there were kids everywhere, so it was pretty easy to climb over the fence of the bottom oval without anyone seeing us. I wanted to know what he was going to do with the snake, but he wouldn't say. Just grinned. He was dead casual. The bell rang and I had Science, dunno what he had, so we went to class. Then after about half an hour the evacuation bell went. We all got hustled out onto the oval but we couldn't work out why we'd all been evacuated or where the problem was. The office staff were out there too. All in a group, looking really jittery. We had to stay out there all afternoon.'

'I'm guessing Snake released the snake somewhere.'

Tobias laughed. 'Sure did! That cunning little rat had sneaked up and let the snake go in the office area. Scared the pants off them all! We had to wait out there until a snake catcher came. The fools didn't realise they had a ready-made snake catcher already enrolled! Snake was laughing fit to bust the whole afternoon. Apparently, the snake wound up in the principal's office. God, it was a laugh.'

Tobias laughed at the memory. Hadley grinned indulgently.

'Not a bad yarn, but back to now. Tobe, you're in a world of trouble, bro. I think you need to get outta town for a bit.'

'What d'ya mean? I didn't give anything to that cop, kept my mouth shut.' Tobias winced when he heard the whine in his voice.

'She could tell, mate. You were strung out like an elephant on a trapeze. Ya gotta go. And it's gotta be interstate, make it harder for them to get you back if they decide to have another look at you. I can hold them off here. Remember, you're on that damned bond. Can't put a foot wrong or you'll be in the slammer.'

Tobias shuddered dramatically. 'Don't say that!'

'Gotta face facts, bro.' Hadley shrugged. 'You sure Snake didn't say anything about where he was taking that woman?'

'Nah. I told you. We just shared a joint and she started making a noise, so he wanted to get going.'

'Did he actually *say* he was going to kill her?'

'No, he just told me how we could dispose of the body.'

'Bloody cold-hearted sod.'

'Yeah, Snake and Feral are both pretty tough.' Tobias reached for his drink.

'No!' Hadley's harsh word made Tobias jump. Hadley came to a sudden decision. 'No more drink. Gotta have you sober. You're driving out of town starting as soon as you pack a bag.'

'What? Where?' Tobias hated that he couldn't handle stress as well as Hadley seemed to.

'Go to Brisbane. They got a good nightlife there, or the Gold Coast. You got plenty of money, just take a holiday. Find out if life's any good up there.'

Tobias leaned back, head tilted, half-closed eyes on the ceiling. 'Yeah. Yeah, I reckon you might have a point, mate. A holiday. Very appealing idea.' Then the grin that had been growing on his face faded. 'But I gotta start doing these community hours,' he said glumly.

'Crap! I forgot about that. Lemme think. A week away might be enough. The cops might have found something else to occupy them by then. That'd still give you time to get the hours done.'

Hadley jumped up, grabbing his keys. 'Let's go. Take your car, fill the tank and meet me at your place.'

Tobias stood up more slowly. 'I'm not sure ...'

'Get going! Now! You know it's for the best. I'll see you in twenty minutes. Hurry up!'

In a very short space of time, Hadley had chivvied his brother onto the road. He waved briefly as Tobias drove off up the street and heaved a relieved sigh. *That fool is so irresponsible. Oh well, I've told him to stay in touch with me and not let anyone know where he is. That's all I can do.* Shrugging, he belted himself in his car and drove back downtown to Tyche.

Tobias was nervous to be leaving the known and loved surroundings of his hometown. He hadn't spent a great deal of time away on his own. As he passed the open road sign, he accelerated, enjoying the speed. The countryside flashed past. Carefully managed paddocks dotted with horses and contented cattle alternated with grey-green eucalypt scrub. Gradually the sense of freedom generated by the road stretching before him brought on a strong feeling of release. Tobias felt like yelling. As the road rose in a winding curve, he wound down the window and bellowed. The wind tore through his hair and cooled his face. He roared until his throat hurt. He hadn't felt so straightforwardly free in a long time.

CHAPTER 10

Elise felt as if she'd been walking forever. She was pleased that so far, her makeshift shoes were doing the job and her feet weren't hurting ... *but oh, this walking is so boring! No phone, no way of telling the time, no music to help pass each dusty step.* She had tried to estimate the distance she'd travelled. She guessed on the safe side she might cover a metre every time her right foot stepped forward. All she had to do was to count that action a thousand times and that was a kilometre covered. Sounded like a simple process. She had noted a large tree and hoped that she would still be able to see it by the time she reached a thousand. Then, she forgot how many hundreds she was up to. She frowned in frustration and started over, noting an unused laneway as a landmark and hoping it would be visible after she counted a thousand. This time, she opened out the fingers on her left hand and closed one into her fist every time she reached a hundred steps. After her fist was entirely closed that was five hundred. Then, she opened a finger each time she reached a hundred. When her fingers were all opened out again, *Wow! A thousand!* She looked back hoping to see the driveway. *Oh great! Didn't even notice going round that curve! Still, if the driveway is beyond that curve, then a kilometre is a fair distance.* She decided it was easier to monitor her progress by simply locating a landmark ahead and then cheering herself on when she reached it. Without having to concentrate on counting, she was free to take in the scenery. It was clear that there was no farming along this road. The paddocks were unkempt, and fences in places were starting to droop. Scrubby regrowth was starting to blur the clean pastures that Elise was accustomed to on her way to the horse stud west of town where her cousin, Silvio, lived with his wife.

Elise saw a small mob of kangaroos enjoying the ungrazed grass. The distant, blue-hazed hills rose smoothly, tree lines showing the gullies and streams. She had a sense of desolation and was unsure whether that was because she herself felt desolate or whether the country truly was desolate and abandoned. The whole of her walk had passed so far undisturbed by a passing car or human being. Once, she heard the distant sound of a jet, and looking up, traced its trail far up in the sky.

Her mind drifted as she plodded along. *Who was responsible for putting me in this situation? Was it to do with my latest job or was it unrelated? Has Diego missed me? Are the police looking for me?* She wondered if all the derelict farms on this road were completely abandoned. She remembered Hartseig Road being mentioned for her disposal, and she couldn't help shuddering again in horror. *Where is that road? Am I near it?* She missed her creature comforts, longed for a hot shower, craved a steaming coffee and a doughnut. *Whoa, steady there, girl. Absolutely no thinking about what you miss. That way lies insanity!*

Suddenly she wailed out loud. 'Noooooo! I left my shoe behind!' *How could I forget my beautiful shoe?* She recalled leaving it on the kitchen bench while she packed for her exit. Then being careful to remember to go to the loo and fill her water bottles, she had walked out without her remaining blue shoe. *Goodness knows what happened to the other one. Oh well, I'm not going back for a shoe, no way.*

Elise padded gently along. She'd taken her time eating a carrot and nibbling through a very sour apple in hopes that eating slowly would make her feel full. She kept having sips of water and had refilled one bottle at a stream that passed under the road. She felt as if she was managing not to overdo the unaccustomed exercise while still making progress. She kept scanning the countryside for buildings where she could either ask for help or if no one was there, camp for the night. She was heading towards the sun and noted it dropping towards the horizon. *Need to start looking for somewhere to stop for the night,* she thought.

✳   ✳   ✳

Ben left the doctor's surgery after his appointment and

glanced at the time. *No point in going back to the station,* he thought, and turned his car towards home. He drove carefully into his driveway, pulled on the handbrake and climbed out. He pressed the 'lock' button.

'Hey, young Ben.' The creaky voice of his neighbour intruded on Ben's drifting thoughts as he pocketed his keys. He straightened, turning towards the divide between the two properties. The grizzled old man barely stood higher than the fence, blue-veined hands gripping the tops of the palings.

'How are you, Mr Cameron?'

A gnarled old finger beckoned him over. 'Don't want to be shoutin' this for all and sundry to hear.' The old man lowered his voice to a rasping whisper.

'I'm all ears, Mr Cameron.' Ben kept his voice respectfully quiet as he walked over to the bent old man.

'You know I go and visit Lizzie every day, just for a chat and a catch-up, and a bit of peace.' Ben nodded. The old chap had lost his wife a couple of months ago and he made a daily visit to the cemetery to tidy her headstone and quietly commune with his departed beloved.

'Odd thing happened, Ben.'

'Go on,' Ben encouraged.

'Well, even though there are paths all crisscrossing the cemetery for people to drive to the graves, I always park my car out the front. I walk in. That's my bit of exercise so I can truthfully tell Lizzie, I'm walking every day.'

Ben smiled.

'She used to nag me something dreadful about staying active. Anyway, I walk in. I brush off leaves from the headstone. I take her flowers every week and I pick out the dead ones each day or toss the lot when they're done.'

Ben nodded, masking his impatience at the lonely old man's ramble. He wondered how long this was going to take and hoped it would be worth listening to.

'So, when that's done, I sit on the bench under the big shady tree, just talkin' to Lizzie in my head.' He paused, remembering. 'You know, it's quite dark under there and if I sit still, I don't reckon I'd be easy to spot. So, yesterday, this car drives slowly along the path. Pulls up about thirty metres away. No one gets out or does anything. Few minutes later, a van pulls up quietly behind it.'

Ben's heart rate quickened, and his interest sharpened. He could hear the wheeze in the old chap's chest.

'Got those black windows, you can't see anything inside. Bloke from the first car gets out, walks back and gets in the van. They sit in the car five or ten minutes. Then the fella returns to his car and they both drive quietly away. No fuss. I thought it was a bit strange. What do you make of that, young Ben? You bein' a policeman ... surely you'd have a few ideas about that.'

Ben certainly did have a few ideas about that, but none that he cared to share with the old man. It seemed someone was using the cemetery as an unobtrusive meeting place. He quickly thought it over. The mention of the van was very interesting. Ben didn't want to put old Mr Cameron in any danger by enlisting his help but on the other hand, this could be something worth following up.

'What sort of van was it? Do you know, Mr Cameron?'

'White, fairly new. I'm not up on all the makes these days.'

'Did you get a number plate?'

The old man looked stricken. 'Never thought of that, mate, sorry.'

'What about the car? Anything to distinguish it?'

'Well, Ben, it was a real flash silver BMW, new, very shiny. Personalised plates, the first letter was a T.'

This sounds most intriguing, thought Ben. 'Do you go to the cemetery at the same time each day, Mr Cameron?' He kept his voice calm despite his inner excitement.

'Not always. Depends what I'm doing. If I've got shopping to do, I go in the afternoon. I usually stay an hour or so.'

'What time were you there yesterday?'

'Late morning. I stopped in after Seniors' pottery.'

'You park on the east side outside the main gate on O'Rourke Road?'

'Yeah. Lizzie is just about in the middle and that lane behind the cemetery isn't sealed and it's rough. So, I stay away from that.'

'Did these two cars come from O'Rourke Road, or the laneway?'

'They went through. Both came from O'Rourke Road and then drove out to the laneway. I guess so they didn't have to turn around.'

'Can you see the laneway from your bench? Any idea which way they went when they left?'

'Nah, 'fraid not. The trees along that section are thick. I've no idea whether they went left or right.'

Ben thought quickly. Maybe that was a regular meeting spot. If the cars drove out into the laneway, maybe he could take a drive through the cemetery tomorrow and see if the meeting was repeated – who they were or at least get their registration numbers and try to identify them that way. Depending on who they were, Mr Cameron's information could be very helpful.

'Well, Mr Cameron, that is quite interesting. But I want you to keep it between you and me. The thing is, they're probably not just out there discussing the weekend footy scores. Don't go drawing attention to yourself because they could be violent if they think you've noticed them. I think I'll do a couple of random drives through the cemetery and out into the laneway tomorrow, try to see if it happens again. You did the right thing telling me about it.'

The old man grinned delightedly. He was proud to have a policeman for a neighbour and thrilled that he may have been helpful.

* * *

Tobias drove his silver BMW into the small township of Blandford, a mere three-quarters of an hour north of Muswellbrook. His euphoria had faded, to be replaced by feelings of resentment. *It's not up to Hadley to tell me what to do. I can take care of myself.* He stopped outside a service station and went inside looking for a snack and a drink.

Returning to the car, he didn't immediately resume his journey. He sipped his drink and hungrily shoved chips in his mouth. The more he thought about it, the less he liked the idea of Hadley giving him orders. He didn't want to go to Brisbane or the Gold Coast. He looked around at the hedges, the paddocks, and the wide-spreading eucalypts, and listened to the birds through the open window. He liked the familiarity of it all. He wanted to stay close to home. Nervously, he acknowledged that Hadley was right about him needing to stay away from the cops, but he felt like he shouldn't get too far from the support of his friends. *What if I got a job on some farm? I could use another name. Then if anything happened in town, I could get back quickly. That damned investigator will have to be found or she'll die.* Tobias screwed his face up in disgust. *Need to think where Snake might have taken her. Where did I tell him to dump her? Oh yes, Hartseig Road, those log piles, that was it! Where the hell is that from here?* He took out his phone and keyed the name into the Maps application. *Oh, there! On the way to, what's that place there? Wheeler? Never heard of it. Maybe I'd better go and see that Snake didn't take her straight to the log piles, kill her and dump her. It's getting late, though. I won't be able to search the log piles in the dark.*

Finally reaching a decision, Tobias turned his car around and drove south. He obeyed the speed limits, being cautiously law-abiding, determined now to stay close to home but out of the eyes of the police. His earlier euphoria and resentment both gave way to some rare prudence. He decided to stay at a motel in Scone and search the log piles in the morning. Then he'd try to get a job on a farm, using a fake name. He'd try out the name at the motel and pay cash. He spent the remainder of the short drive considering suitable names.

In Scone, the Royal Hotel Motel sign beckoned to Tobias with a welcoming glow. He drove into a side street and parked carefully. Enquiries revealed that there was a room available, and he booked in under the name of Trevor Laverty. No suspicious eyebrows were raised, in fact the barmaid who gave him his room key was friendly and helpful.

'After you dump your stuff in your room, come down and have a drink. Dinner is served from six o'clock.'

Tobias followed her instructions, noting that although the room was old-fashioned, it was clean and quiet. The shared bathroom was down the end of the corridor. He felt his tension ease and began to look forward to a beer and a steak. *Best stay away from the ganja, don't want to draw attention to myself,* he thought. *And maybe I really do need to keep my head a bit clearer. Got to find that woman and got to find a job. Okay, Mr Trevor Laverty, you're a clean-living rural bloke now, not a drug dealing tattoo parlour owner. Time to get into character.* Tobias squared his shoulders and went downstairs, hoping that his new clean-living persona would come up with some ideas by tomorrow.

✻   ✻   ✻

No such luxury awaited Elise. She trudged on, eyes raking the paddocks for buildings. Nothing showed and she spent her time planning her night-time preparations; had to keep her mind occupied or she'd start really stressing. *I'll just go up this little hill and round the corner and see what I can see. If there isn't a building or house, I'll find some scrub to bed down in and get comfortable before it gets dark. I really want a shower, I must smell terrible, especially since I hadn't even had a shower when they took me. Oh God, was it really only Tuesday? Yesterday? Mustn't lose track of the days.*

She plodded on, one foot in front of the other, still seeing no sign of any farm buildings. *Perhaps I was a bit hasty leaving that farmhouse? No! Believe in yourself. You're heading away from danger and towards help.*

CHAPTER 11

'Oh my god, it's hardly even light!' Ava moaned to Karah Nester as they stood, shivering slightly in the cool morning air, with the rest of the students waiting for the bus.

'Mmm, six o'clock is a bit rude for a start. But I'm looking forward to it. I think it will be a really interesting day and we can sleep in the bus on the way,' Karah replied.

Their lecturer, Pelle, had a mate working for National Parks and Wildlife at Narrabri. His area included Mount Kaputar National Park, which was a long drive to the northwest of Muswellbrook. He had agreed to notify Pelle when he planned to hold a practical session on fire planning and fuel management. Pelle wanted his students to experience firsthand the technicalities entailed in managing Australian bush with consideration to flora, fauna and humans. It is a delicate balance controlling accumulated dried vegetation with supervised burns to prevent large bushfires, while protecting the animals and plants alike. The Mount Kaputar region is famous not just for the variety of eucalypts and other dry rainforest plants, but also for the giant fluorescent pink slug which inhabits a single mountain peak in the park. Pelle reasoned that there would be something to interest everyone on this field trip. The class was travelling by coach to Mount Kaputar where they were to participate in a series of practical demonstrations including hazard reduction burns.

Each student had a backpack with all they would need for the day in the way of food and drink, as they'd been advised there were no shops on the mountain. Along with their food requirements they had the usual sunscreen, hats and jackets, in case it was cold on the mountain. At its highest, Mount Kaputar rose almost 1,500 metres above sea level. Because of its height, the weather around the mountain could be very unpredictable. Some of the more conscientious students carried notebooks, while others were content to take pictorial notes with their phones.

With a hiss of brakes, the bus slowed to a halt and the sleepy students climbed aboard.

* * *

Out west, near the village of Wheeler, Graham Buckley was a contented man. He and Jan had heard that morning from their twin sons that they had found somewhere to live in London and one of them already had a job. Graham wasn't happy that they'd gone so far away but he was pleased that things seemed to be going smoothly for them. *Still,* he mused, *we've got Ted and Rebecca and the three littlies nice and handy in Muswellbrook.* His son Ted was married to Elise's sister Rebecca. Ted had his own real estate business in town. Graham and Jan understood their twins' need to have an adventure on their own, away from their parents. They'd earned it. They were good sons and had made it through high school with a minimum of trouble, both working on the farm to earn the money they were spending now on a working holiday in England for their 'gap year'. Graham had held some conversations with his wife about the possibility they could get away themselves a bit more often in future. There were just a few more things he had to streamline on the farm so they could leave it for longer periods. He walked through to Jan's sunny studio. She made leather goods, beautifully tooled, hand-stitched leather handbags, belts, purses, and hand-bound computer cases. Her braided leather whips were in demand all over Australia, as well as Canada and the US. He inhaled deeply. He loved the leather smell, mingled with her light floral perfume. Glancing at the handbag she was working on, he leaned over resting his hands on her shoulders.

'That binding is so neat and even. I don't know how you do it, love. It's beautiful. I'm going up to the top paddock. Noticed some broken wires in the fence. Not a big job. Should be back for a cuppa round ten-thirty or so.'

She raised her face for his goodbye kiss, smiled and said, 'I'll put the kettle on about then.'

He took his hat from the hook by the back door, bent to pull on his elastic-sided boots and whistled. 'Coming, Blade?'

The black and tan kelpie ran up, wagging his tail joyfully. A trip with his master was always a delight for him, new scents on the wind, maybe some stock work; at the very least, the chance to chase his tail in the paddock when they stopped. Graham made sure he had his wire strainers, fencing pliers and a coil of spare wire in the tray of the handy little all-terrain vehicle he affectionately called Alf. He believed Alf was a step up from a quad bike because he could carry quite a large variety of equipment in the tray. He'd even brought a sick calf home in it once. If there was a job requiring two people, Alf was much more comfortable for Jan to travel in, too, although in their early days on the farm, they'd both used horses for most tasks.

He set off, as usual letting instinct and long familiarity guide him while his eyes roamed back and forth across the paddocks checking for problems or just savouring the view. As he drove along the ridge, his eyes dropped down the slope on his left. Roughly two hundred metres away in the valley were the log piles he had pushed up some months ago. He reminded himself it would soon be time to burn them, they'd certainly have dried out by now. *Wait! What's that?* He slowed Alf, frowning. Someone was clambering on one of the piles of felled timber. A silver car was parked out on the road. Graham stopped, switching off the engine, and Blade excitedly jumped down.

'Stay!' Graham commanded the dog. The dog crouched obediently.

He watched for a while. He could only see one person, a man, searching the log pile he had climbed on. As Graham watched, the man scrambled off that pile, walked to the next and climbed onto it, resuming his search. *What the hell is he doing?*

A fence ran along the side of the valley between Graham and the paddock the log piles were in. Quickly he started Alf, and barely waiting for Blade to jump back on, he gunned the engine, heading for the connecting gate about five hundred metres further on.

Tobias, crawling across logs, heard the engine and glanced up. He was reassured that the little vehicle was up on the hilltop and moving away from him. He quickly jumped off the logs he was on and went to the next pile, not really enjoying the search but determined to try to sort out where the woman was.

Suddenly he realised he could hear the engine much closer. The last thing he wanted was to have to answer questions from a potentially angry farmer. He crouched and scrambled off the log pile, keeping it between himself and the approaching vehicle. He ran for the fence and vaulted over it, heading for his car.

Graham lost sight of the intruder behind the logs and overshot the pile Tobias had jumped off. He did a quick U-turn around the end of the pile and was just in time to see the man scrambling to get into his car. Graham cursed under his breath and raced towards the car.

Tobias jammed the key in the ignition and, revving the engine madly, he took off before he'd even got his door closed or his seatbelt fastened.

Graham coasted to a halt, frowning. *What was that guy up to?* He sighed regretfully as he realised that he hadn't even noted the number plate. It looked so simple on the television shows, witnesses always noticed details like that. But Graham had been so intent on simply catching up to the man, he hadn't thought of anything else. Blade jumped down and began coursing around, sniffing, engrossed in his own doggie heaven. Graham slowly tracked around the log pile he'd seen the man on. He climbed on the logs but couldn't see anything out of the ordinary. He checked another pile with the same result. He checked a third pile, wondering if the guy had intended to light a fire but he could find no evidence of any tampering.

Deep in thought, he called the dog and resumed his way to the broken fence.

❊   ❊   ❊

Tobias sped away, his heart pounding. It took him a while to realise that the farmer couldn't very easily follow him because he would have to find a gate to get out onto the road. Gradually he eased his foot off the accelerator and his breathing returned to normal. *Bloody hell, that was close!*

Travelling once again at the speed limit, he was determined to be a law-abiding citizen and conveniently forgot he was just guilty of trespassing. Tobias looked around at the well-tended paddocks and the peacefully grazing stock. A white sign ahead advised the speed limit written in bold black numerals surrounded by a red circle. Tobias obediently slowed to sixty, looking with interest at the scattered houses and the attractive old church in the village of Wheeler. He'd slept well at the hotel in Scone but hadn't felt like eating before he set off. Now that his rushing heart and adrenalin had settled down, he realised he was hungry.

Tobias slowed to a halt in front of the general store. In the store, he selected a packaged sandwich and an iced coffee. He walked slowly around the store and came to a halt in front of a notice board. Two words jumped out at him 'Gardener Wanted'. *Hey, how good is that? That's a job I know I can do.* Tobias smirked at the memory of his success growing marijuana. He read the name and address. Burt Bunrack, Croham.

'How do I find Croham?' he asked the storekeeper while he paid for his snack.

'Follow the right fork in the road. It'll be easy to see

– lion-topped pillars and Croham painted in gold letters on a white background. You can't miss it.'

'Thanks, mate.'

* * *

Elise had not fared as well as Tobias when it came to her night's accommodation. No farmhouse was to be seen in her lonely progression along the dusty road. Eventually, she realised that if she was to have enough daylight to make herself as comfortable as possible for the night, she must abandon her search for a farmhouse and look instead for a grove of trees close by the road that might provide some shelter. Although she was pleased that her feet had coped with the walk, she felt miserable and alone. Her stomach rumbled, not content with the diet of raw vegetables and fruit. She looked carefully at the clear sky, realising she had to rely on that or get rained on during the night out in the open. She was grateful that the weather was reasonably warm.

Putting her water bottles safely against the butt of a tree, she stacked some solid branches around them to prevent the bottles from being knocked over and to protect her food sack. She gathered bark, leaves and some bracken fern and pushed them roughly into a bed shape. Elise settled her back against another tree and took stock. She was surprised at how much planning was required to live in this very simple way:

'shoes' to refill with grass, a 'bed' to be made, 'evening meal' to plan. *Mum would be stunned to see me being so practical.* A wry smile twisted her mouth. *I'm just so lonely, couldn't live like this. Need to be able to talk to people or I'll go mad.* She had tried singing out loud to pass the time during the day, but she'd felt a bit silly serenading the birds and kangaroos. She chose two vegetables from her store and ate them slowly. Then she drank some water. Looking around, she decided that the soft grass beyond the trees would be ideal to refill her 'shoes'. She collected a large armful of grass and re-stuffed her shoes. *Now, do I wear my shoes to bed? I suppose so. Easier to get going in a hurry if necessary.*

Elise wasn't scared to be alone in the bush. She knew the worst that could threaten her would possibly be a fox, but she reasoned that this was cattle country rather than sheep country and foxes were to be found in greater numbers where sheep grazed. She knew there were wild dogs and dingoes in the bush but again, she guessed they would be unlikely to be in the area where she found herself because there was so little in the way of food for them there.

She allowed herself a little moment to bemoan the lack of a hot shower, glass of wine, someone to talk to. Then she gave herself a mental shake and put her woes behind her. In the fading daylight, she tied her new 'shoes' on her feet, wrapped herself in her curtain blanket and laid down on her 'bed'. It was not comfortable in the conventional sense and the bark rattled noisily when she moved. She looked at the sky, locating the bright evening star through the sparse eucalypt canopy above and almost immediately fell deeply asleep. She woke a few times through the night but dozed off again quite quickly, grateful that all the unaccustomed walking had tired her out thoroughly.

The last time she woke, early birds were stirring, and the sky was lightening to the east. She stretched, assessing how her body was dealing with the rigours of living rough. Aside from overall stiffness, she felt surprisingly good. Alas, that feeling was not to last. Muscles and bones were fine, but her stomach abruptly began to rebel loudly and uncomfortably against the meagre diet of raw fruit and vegetables. Elise was forced to leap up and dash away from her camp to deal with the problem. *Yuck. That was an unexpected drawback.* She opted for a breakfast of water only, to give her stomach a chance to settle.

Deciding there was no point in lingering, Elise gathered her belongings and set off once again. She would have been cheered to know that she had covered seven kilometres on her walk the previous day. Sadly, her progress was to be much slower today on account of her cramping stomach and the need to stop frequently.

* * *

'Hey boss, we got the DNA results on that blood from the van and it's a match for Elise. Clicks used the toothbrush from Elise's bathroom. So, I'd say we got the van. Now all we have to do is find out where it's been.'

'Wow, that's good news, Ben! I'll forgive the omission of a polite "good morning".' Kaylee smiled, cheered that they had some progress.

Ben pulled a face. 'And, listen to this. I also have a feeling my old neighbour saw the van at the cemetery. Possibly using the area as a quiet place to meet unobserved. He said the van pulled up and so did a silver BMW. And the silver BMW had personalised plates, the first letter being T! I ran it through the database and added an L for Lardner and guess what? Bingo! Perfect match!'

'Wow, Ben, that's great. I hope you thanked your observant old neighbour very sincerely. So, it looks like Tobias and Eric met at the cemetery to create their plan for a kidnapping. Very useful. I rang that guy, Patrick Carlton, brother of Eric. He and his parents are with Eric but there's no change in his condition. Doctors are talking in terms of later rather than sooner for him to recover sufficiently to be brought out of the coma. And even then, they cannot say whether he will be capable of remembering anything helpful.'

Ben's face fell, then he brightened. 'Well, boss. Look on the bright side: finding Elise will be down to sheer hard detecting on the part of our fabulous team.'

Kaylee grimaced, thinking that if they didn't get a lucky

break, they might be too late finding her.

'You *do* love a challenge, don't you, Ben! Task for today is as I said yesterday: you and I re-interview Tobias. A team's to be allocated to tracking down Eric's friends to question and see if he let slip any clues about Elise. See if we can get what we need without bothering the Carltons too much. They must be very anxious about their son. Probably don't need to add to their troubles at this stage by suggesting that he's a kidnapper.'

'Will we start at Tobias' flat or the tattoo shops?'

'My guess is he's not an early riser. Let's see if we can surprise him at home. Meet me in the carpark. I've a couple of quick errands in-house while you detail the team with their allotted tasks.'

In a short time, they were driving to Tobias' address. Ben knocked, waited, then hammered on the door. He turned to Kaylee and shrugged in frustration. She gestured with her phone. Ben dialled the number and listened carefully at the door to see if he could hear it ringing inside. He dialled a second time and still had no response.

Back in the car, he said shortly, 'Your turn.'

'With pleasure,' Kaylee grinned.

Hadley rolled over in bed and reached for his phone. 'Hello?'

The cheerful voice of Detective Sergeant Kaylee Bradshaw jolted him out of the last of his sleep.

'We're at your brother's place. He's not answering the door or his phone. Have you any idea where we can find him?'

'I'm guessing you mean Tobias, not Lex,' he growled.

'Oh yes. We definitely mean Tobias. He wasn't very forthcoming yesterday and we think he might have a bit more information to share.'

Hadley let out a silent sigh of relief and cleared his throat. 'I haven't seen Tobias since yesterday arvo, and he didn't share his plans with me.'

Kaylee thanked him and ended the call with a disgusted grunt. In reply to Ben's raised eyebrows, she shrugged. 'He hasn't seen him. So, I guess now we'll have to traipse round the whole family trying to find him. What a tiresome job.'

'Wait a bit. What's wrong with working backwards? Let's have a more in-depth chat with the Nester family, the men in particular. We could try to find out why they wanted the Lardners investigated. Might give us some insight.'

'You know, Benny-boy, you're not just a pretty face! That's a great idea.'

Kaylee waited for him to fasten his seatbelt, then drove calmly to Golden Motors garage.

CHAPTER 12

Rhea mechanically offered Evander her cheek to kiss as he passed her on his way through the kitchen to the laundry and then into the garage. She heard the roller door rumble up in response to his press on the remote control.

'See you later,' she said more from convention than because she thought he was listening or would respond. She sighed, reflecting that their relationship was in a very sad state and wondering what to do about it. She pushed the thought to the back of her mind and walked to the bathroom to apply her make-up and do her hair. Cleo would be here soon. She put on her shoes and returned to the kitchen.

'Millie, come here sweetheart. I'm going to be out all day, so you can have a day in the backyard. Come on, I'll top up your grits. A quiet day won't hurt you and we'll have a quick play when I get home.' She lovingly ruffled the velvet-soft ears, enjoying the unquestioning trust in the dog's eyes. She knew Millie would be fine in the garden. She had plenty of toys, a large comfortable kennel, full water dish, butterflies to chase. *I wonder why retrievers love chasing butterflies. Macey did that and Maizie too. Funny gorgeous dogs.*

Her friendship with Cleo Lardner had developed rapidly from coffee after gym sessions to a variety of shared outings. They had so much in common, from an appreciation of music and the arts to a strong sense of humour and readiness to enjoy everything life had to offer. They never seemed to run out of things to share and discuss. They recognised in each other that they were at a crossroads, trying to find a fulfilling activity to occupy themselves now that their children were grown.

Today they were driving to Newcastle to see a visiting art show exploring the human desire to travel. It had a strong appeal for both women, and they had already lightly discussed travelling overseas together. Rhea felt that unless she and Evander managed to get back to their old closeness, he wouldn't miss her if she went on a trip. Cleo was free to plan and go whenever she felt like it but was still somewhat lacking in self-confidence to travel alone. A leisurely lunch would follow the art exhibition and possibly some retail therapy. *A girl can never have too many clothes,* Rhea thought with a small smile. Her smile widened when she heard the beep of a car in her driveway. Grabbing her handbag and dark glasses, she left the house, carefully locking the door.

'You look great,' Cleo commented by way of greeting.

'We both do, thanks to that slave driver in the gym.'

'Yeah, he works us hard. But he sure gets results. You ready?' Rhea nodded and Cleo purred her Mercedes out of the driveway, turning to the south to join the highway to Newcastle.

The drive took no time at all, their animated conversation covered many topics and before they knew it, Cleo was looking for a park near the art gallery. The exhibition was all they expected and more, covering so many variations on the travel theme; their imaginations were fired.

'Oh, wow! What a great way to spend a morning. I loved that! Do you know it's lunchtime already?'

'Yes. I was so rapt and drawn along by each new piece that I didn't even think of stopping for coffee. What about that huge painting of the tall ship? The stormy sky was the perfect thunderous blue-grey. Nearly made me feel seasick!'

Cleo smiled. 'Well, we should start thinking of lunch. I'm pretty sure we clocked up a few thousand steps in there and I'm famished as well as ready to rest my legs a bit.'

'Got anywhere in mind?'

'There's a café in Darby Street that one of the ladies at the gym was talking about. Let's see if we can find it.'

Soon, they were seated by the huge windows looking out into the busy sunny street. An attentive waiter quickly took their orders and brought a water bottle and glasses to their table.

They chatted on sharing their impressions of the various artworks they had seen.

Then Cleo suddenly said, 'You want to know something odd, Rhea?'

Cleo's friend looked at her with interest tinged with concern. 'Sure. Tell me.'

'Yesterday a policewoman came round, asking me questions about a missing woman.'

Rhea's eyes widened in shock. 'God! Same here!'

Cleo sat back, staring at Rhea in surprise. 'Now that's really weird! She asked me if I knew anything about a private investigator, said the woman was missing and they were concerned for her.'

'That's exactly what they said to me. What could that have to do with either of us? Have you been using an investigator?'

'No, not at all. Have you?'

'No. But Evander has been very touchy lately, not talking to me about anything. Seems to spend more time with the boys at the garage than in his shop.'

Cleo sighed. 'I don't see much of the kids anymore. Lex drops in occasionally, but he's got a new girlfriend and he's spending all his time with her. She's another student, I think he said she's studying environmental science.'

'Karah's doing that. Wait! Oh God, how could I be so vague? Lex! Lex is the name of her boyfriend!'

'You're kidding!' Cleo let out a delighted laugh. 'Our kids are dating!'

'Oh, that's priceless. We become friends and so do our kids. How lovely. Still, I guess it's not really that surprising, our town isn't that big.'

With yet another topic to dissect and speculate on, their lunch passed very quickly, and the subject of the missing woman was easily forgotten.

*   *   *

Evander was frowning as he drove to his shop. *What happened to Rhea and me?* He missed the easy closeness they had shared for most of their marriage. Vaguely he realised that he had neglected their relationship. The issue over his reaction to Rhea's painting had blown into something huge. He regretted having to share the whole family feud thing about the Lardners because Rhea's reaction had been so negative. He was also slightly ashamed of clinging to the past, not moving with the times and forgetting about the stupid feud. And now Karah was dating one of them! He knew only too well from frequent clashes with his stubborn daughter over the years that banning her from seeing the guy would have the opposite effect. *Maybe I should have told Rhea I organised the private investigator to look into that Lardner and his family. She would have seen red and we'd have had another row. Why is Karah so damned strong-minded? Why can't she have picked any other guy than a Lardner? And what the hell was it with the police investigating the disappearance of the PI? Bloody Ladas or Lardners, always trouble whatever way you look at them.*

On impulse, Evander decided not to open the shop today,

there was nothing pressing to attend to. He decided to put a 'closed' sign in the window and hang out with his sons at the garage, see how things were going there.

Damien and Christos were glad to see their father and accepted without comment his reasons for being at the garage. They had also been questioned by the police about the missing woman and were mystified why the police would think they were connected to her in any way. They had no time to discuss it with their father. They had bigger problems to occupy them with both Snake and Feral off work and two urgent jobs demanding their attention.

A tow truck had arrived from Sydney very early that morning carrying a BMW and an Audi. They had quickly unloaded the vehicles and moved them deep into the workshop away from prying eyes. The vehicles were both in need of a new paint job and new identities. Damien had already organised the resale of the 'refreshed' vehicles in Queensland and was impatient not to have them in his garage any longer than necessary. The arrival of the police and their questions had rattled his calm, leaving him feeling rather exposed. Early on, when his father had installed him and Christos as managers, he'd been surprised when his father outlined his plans for the garage. Damien thought the garage showed such a healthy profit simply because it catered to wealthy car owners. He hadn't known the previous owner had been making a tidy nest egg on the side by re-birthing stolen cars and selling them on. Evander had realised the potential for making money and encouraged Damien to expand the illegal aspect of the business.

The system was quite straightforward. Their contact in Sydney notified when a truck would be arriving carrying stolen cars. Damien quickly organised the respray, the false numberplate and fake vehicle identification number. Knowing the car would soon be reregistered in Queensland, he was confident the false plates wouldn't draw any negative attention. When the cars were ready, he contacted his link in Brisbane who organised buyers. Damien liked to ship the cars overnight, trusting in the cover of darkness and the reduced presence of highway police. He had confidence that Snake and Feral kept quiet about the activities in the garage because he paid them well over the going rate for spray painters and mechanics. They were good workers who didn't ask too many questions.

Now things seemed to be getting complicated. His father was sometimes remote and distracted, Snake was in a coma, Feral was with Snake, and Damien was short two workers. He decided he and Christos would have to work long into the next few nights to get the cars to Brisbane in the time arranged. *And what the heck is it with us being questioned about this missing woman?*

❅   ❅   ❅

Tobias ate his snack in the car, enjoying the peaceful atmosphere of the little village. Even the small groups of children heading to school were calmly walking along without the usual boisterous skirmishes children sometimes engage in as a matter of course. He dropped the empty food container and drink bottle in the footwell on the passenger side of his car and followed the directions he'd been given in the shop. The road went beside a creek with black boulders glistening in the spray as the water rushed around them. Short vivid green shrubs fringed both sides of the creek.

Croham was, as the shop owner had said, hard to miss. The lion-topped pillars were elegant and eye-catching. He turned in between them and coasted gently to a halt in front of a long, low white house. It had a red tiled roof and scarlet bougainvillea flowering brilliantly. Further along, behind the house, he could see a man walking along the rows of an orderly market garden. Beyond, black cattle dotted the white-fenced paddocks. The overall impression was of a well-run and productive organisation. Tobias felt his spirits lift. *I could enjoy working here.*

He walked towards the man, who had seen the car pull up and had changed direction to see who had arrived.

The two men met at the fence. On closer inspection, Tobias saw an older, stocky man with fierce reddish eyebrows and his right arm in plaster.

'Well, young fella, what can I do fer you?'

'Um, the name's Trevor Laverty. I saw your ad in the shop, for a gardener.'

'Ahh!' Burt gave a satisfied purr. 'I'm Burt Bunrack.' He awkwardly held his plastered arm over the fence. Tobias shook his hand. 'Ya better come in. We can 'ave a talk over a coffee. Knock on the door, the wife's inside. I'll go in the back.'

Following Burt's instructions, Tobias knocked and was greeted by a beautiful dark-haired woman. He introduced himself again.

'Ahh!' Gisella sounded pleased. 'You come just in time! Come in, come in. We really needing help. Come in. I'm Gisella,' she added grandly as an afterthought.

Tobias followed her through the cool, dark hallway to an airy sunroom that ran along the entire length of the house. He was amused at the way they both said, 'Ahh' with such evident relief at his arrival.

'Now young fella,' Burt said when they were seated at the sunroom table with steaming coffees and a plate of almond biscotti. 'Tell us a bit about yerself. As ya can see, I've busted me arm and me and Gisella 'ave to get these vegetables picked regular for the Sydney market. Both gettin' a bit long in the tooth for this caper.'

Tobias had a moment of horror when he realised that he hadn't prepared any sort of fake identity other than his name.

'Um, well, I'm just travelling round really. Picking up work where I can, to fund the next leg of my journey, you know?'

It sounded weak and he knew he could tie himself in knots if he wasn't careful.

'So, you got experience?'

'Ah, pfft,' Gisella cut in. 'Not need experience to pick a few vegetables. Just strong back and ready to work hard.'

'Yeah, pretty much as she said,' Burt growled, not happy with the interruption. 'But we don't want no sloppy work 'ere. Them veg 'as to be in top condition when they arrive in Sydney, or we don't get top dollar.'

A vehicle could be heard pulling up on the gravel out the front.

Burt cocked his head. 'That'll be Silvio,' he said as Gisella jumped up with a delighted crow.

'Oh, hope he bring bambino!' She bustled excitedly to the front door.

Silvio it was. Gisella and Burt's cherished son, bringing with him their even more cherished grandson. Silvio knew there would be no silencing his mum if he didn't bring the baby. Susannah, his wife, was busy working yearlings at the next-door horse stud and was happy for him to take little Oliver off her hands. She knew all too well that the baby would be safe but spoiled rotten by his grandmother and Silvio would be doing little in the way of babysitting.

'Ahh, my boys,' she cooed. 'One so big and handsome and one so small and handsome. Shoo, Silvio, shoo. Go inside to Papa. Let me see my little *caro*. Come, come, piccolo bambino. Come to Nonna.' She expertly took over the task of extricating the baby from his car seat. The baby gurgled, holding out his arms to his doting Nonna and thus wedging himself even more solidly in her heart. Silvio grinned and went inside carrying the bag of baby needs.

'Hey, Dad.'

'Son. This 'ere is Trevor, 'e's interested in the job.'

Silvio looked over the slim young man, taking in his soft shoes and equally soft-looking hands. *Doesn't look like he'll be much use, but I guess we can't afford to be too choosy. I can't be running back and forth all the time.*

Silvio and Susannah both worked at Divine Hayfields, a large horse stud owned by Susannah's stepbrother. Susannah worked mainly with the horses and Silvio attended to the farming, crop planting and maintenance. He was also responsible for the upkeep of all the farm machinery. When he had time, he helped his father out with work in the market garden. Although Burt was getting on in years, his dad was usually self-sufficient. He'd fallen clumsily using the two-wheel tractor, landing heavily across the driving handlebars. Gisella was not a farming partner, her strength was in the bookkeeping and continually upgrading their market contacts in Sydney. Since Burt had broken his arm, it had become more difficult for Silvio to juggle work and the baby, especially as the vegetables needed to be gathered first thing in the morning, at exactly the same time as baby

Oliver was waking up demanding attention. The working relationship with Susannah's stepbrother, Mac, was an amiable one and allowed them considerable flexibility, but even so, Silvio would be glad to have someone working for his father full-time.

'Come out an' 'ave a look round.' Burt stood up and headed out the back door, followed by Silvio and Tobias/ Trevor. Gisella was already engrossed with the placid little eight-month-old.

'Be out in a sec, Dad.'

Silvio paused for a moment, turning to his mother. 'If this guy is working for you, where is he going to stay? You don't know anything about him. I don't like the idea of a total stranger staying in the house with you and Dad.'

Gisella frowned. 'I not think about that. Any spare bedroom in the worker's cottage up at the stud?'

'Yeah, there is a room empty up there just now. Hang on, I'll ring Mac and see if it's okay for Trevor to stay there. You happy to pay for his room or do you want to take it out of his pay?'

'Oh, no problem. We pay. Claim back at tax time. Ring Mac.'

Gisella fed mashed banana to little Oliver, laughing gently at the baby and carefully avoiding his chubby hands reaching for the spoon.

'Right, Mama. Mac says it's okay for Trevor to stay up

there. He'll let Mrs Sullivan know there's one extra to be fed. Tell Trevor how to get there and make sure he's up there by six-thirty. That's when Mrs Sullivan puts the staff dinner on the table. I'd better go and let Dad and Trevor know.'

He lovingly ran his hand over his son's smooth dark head and went outside.

CHAPTER 13

Karah stepped out of the bus and looked around. They were surrounded by tall eucalypts with startling white bark. Thick undergrowth blocked their view after only a short distance. She listened to the birdsong that even her excitedly chattering fellow students couldn't drown out. She had three 'must sees' on her list. One was a koala, and she thought that would be relatively easy to find. The second was the Guthega skink, which she knew would be more difficult because they are very shy. The third thing she was curious to see was a grass tree, commonly called the Black Boy. This hardy, slow-growing plant is well adapted to the dry Australian bush with long slender leaves to minimise water loss. She hoped to see one that was flowering with its long spear-like spike. For some reason, the plant had fascinated her since she first read about it.

'Phew, long trip,' her friend Ava moaned, massaging her neck.

'You need a snack,' Karah commented, eyeing her friend. She knew Ava was prone to low blood sugar and needed to keep snacking all day rather than eating three big meals.

'Right, guys. Listen up,' Pelle called to the group. 'We'll need to stick pretty closely to our schedule today because the National Parks guys have organised a full day for us. So, you've got twenty minutes for a snack and a drink, and a comfort stop. Then we reconvene for our guided tour along the plateau walk. We can learn a lot about the history of the area as well as the plants and wildlife. It's a loop so we'll be back here for lunch. Following lunch, we'll move on Mount Kaputar for the hazard reduction demonstration.'

'Just what you needed. Eat something, Ava. I think I heard that National Parks guy say it's an eight-kilometre track,' Karah advised her friend.

* * *

Elise's walk was becoming torture. Her cramping stomach slowed her pace, and she couldn't come to terms with the lack of company. She tried a monologue detailing the sights, but her progress was so slow, that there were long silences while she waited for some new item of scenery to describe. She paused for another sip of water and hoped nibbling a carrot wouldn't make her protesting stomach worse.

She leaned on a roadside fence post scanning the country while she slowly munched. She felt small and miserable, and tears spilled slowly down her cheeks. 'Well, this is no good,' she said grimly, wiping her face with the back of her hand.

'Pull yourself together. If you start giving in because of a few little setbacks, you'll never make it back to town. Hey, wait, what's that?'

At that moment, the sun shone out from behind a cloud and a distant roof gleamed.

'Woohoo! I see a building! I can do this.' With renewed vigour, Elise started walking again.

* * *

Kaylee pulled up at Golden Motors, carefully parking out of the way. Then the two tall police officers strolled into the office where Evander was seated behind the desk. Damien and Christos straightened from looking over his shoulder at some paperwork. Ben and Kaylee were both instantly struck by a strong sense of tension in the room. Ben thought he detected a degree of wariness in Damien's non-committal greeting.

'How handy to have all three of you here together,' Ben began. 'We want to ask you a few more questions about the missing private investigator.'

'Look,' Damien started quickly, 'I don't think we can add much more, and we are shorthanded here with a number of urgent jobs waiting.'

'Yes, I can understand you'd be a bit pressed with two staff members off,' Kaylee said casually.

Ben noticed the immediate stiffening of Damien's shoulders.

'Yes,' Kaylee added sweetly, 'we know about Eric's accident and his brother needing to take his parents to the hospital.'

The tension in the room increased. Evander regretted not having the chance to brief his sons about his actions. This could go in any direction. He gritted his teeth. 'Perhaps if we just answer their questions, the police will go and let us get on with work,' he rumbled.

'Why did you hire Ms Dean to investigate the Lardner family?'

'They're low-life scum, and my daughter is dating one of them. I think if I found something concrete on them, my daughter could be persuaded that she could make better choices.'

'In what way are they low-life scum? What were you hoping to discover? Which one is your daughter dating? Did you organise for Eric Carlton to abduct Ms Dean?'

All three Nester men jumped as if they'd been stung.

'What?'

'No way!'

'What are you talking about?'

'Yes. I must admit it seemed strange to us that you would hire an investigator and then have her kidnapped. Unless of course you were intending it to look like the Lardners had taken her.'

'Well, you must be off your rocker to think we did it!' Evander said severely. 'You're dead right. Yes, I hired her and yes, I hoped she would find out something damning about them, but her disappearance is a complete mystery to us.'

'So how do you explain one of your staff members having her blood in his vehicle?'

Damien looked from Christos to his father. His father shrugged. Ben, watching their faces, noticed a slow dawning of recognition on Christos' face. 'Do you have something to add to this, Christos?' he asked.

'Um, Snake, I mean Eric, was a year ahead of me at high school, in the same year as Tobias Lardner. They were thick as thieves back then, still best buddies now.'

Evander's black eyebrows lowered into a heavy scowl. Damien looked shocked.

'And is it Tobias Lardner that your daughter is dating?' Kaylee couldn't take her eyes off the interesting variety of expressions across the faces of the three Nester men.

'No, she's dating Lex, the youngest one. He's at uni with her.'

'Did you find out anything from Ms Dean that would have helped you dissuade your daughter from the relationship?'

'No. I'd only just hired her. She hasn't even sent me a preliminary report.'

'Do you have a bathroom I could use?' Kaylee asked suddenly.

'Sure,' Damien responded without thinking. He gestured towards the back of the garage then froze. Kaylee quickly headed from the office through a side door without a glance at Damien. Damien lurched as if to follow her, then jerked to a stop at Evander's raised hand.

'I think we've helped you all we can,' he said slowly. 'If Eric was involved in abducting Ms Dean, he has acted on his own or under someone else's instruction. It's nothing to do with us. I simply hired the woman. That's it.'

'You've been very helpful, thank you.' Ben kept his voice neutral. 'I'll wait at the car for my senior officer to join me and you can get on with your work.'

He walked outside and leaned on the police car, casually surveying the scenery. Within minutes, Kaylee was hurrying towards him, jingling the car keys in her hand.

'Sorry about that,' she said for the benefit of anyone listening, 'sudden call of nature. Let's go.'

In the car, she spoke as she drove off. 'Well, I think you and I need to have a quiet coffee and a recap of all we know.'

'Good idea. Your shout,' Ben responded cheekily.

Kaylee gave him a grinning sidelong glance. 'Ben, just before coffee, can you do a check on these two number plates?' She recited the first one and waited while he keyed in the details.

'Stolen Audi. Reported yesterday morning.'

'And this one?' Again, Kaylee quoted a number plate.

After a pause, Ben said, 'BMW reported stolen sometime during the night before yesterday.'

'Good.' Kaylee smiled her satisfaction. 'Now organise a team to go round and arrest Damien and Christos and Evander for receiving stolen goods. Soon as we stop, I'll organise JP David O'Hara to issue a search warrant. Here we are. What do you want?'

'Just a mug, flat white, thanks boss.'

Kaylee pulled into a carpark and headed into a coffee shop, leaving Ben on the phone.

Back in the car, she handed Ben his coffee. She quickly rang the Justice, outlining her requirements for the search warrant, adding that it was a matter of some urgency for the warrant to be delivered to the police officers who would by then be at Golden Motors.

'You're very calm, considering our progress this morning,' Ben commented.

'We *had* to start making some progress by now, so I feel some satisfaction, yes. The Nesters didn't shed any light, other than the father is a suspicious controlling man. And I'm still very concerned about Elise Dean.'

'Me too, poor woman. So let me get this clear: The Nesters had two stolen vehicles in their garage and our lads are on their way now to deal with that. Good thinking, by the way, suddenly needing a bathroom. Damien almost had a fit when he realised what he'd done, casually indicating that you could go out through the workshop. The tension in that office certainly rose a notch or two!' He smiled at the memory.

Kaylee allowed herself a smug smile as well. 'The cars were well towards the back and half concealed by a couple of other cars, not obvious to the casual observer.'

Ben nodded and continued, 'We are now almost positive that Eric "Snake" Carlton was involved in the kidnap of Elise Dean. He is unconscious and in no position to answer any of our questions. It is *probable* that Tobias Lardner enlisted Eric to help him with the kidnap. He is not answering his phone and his whereabouts are unknown. He claims not to know where Elise is. Lying? Was Eric acting alone? Where to from here?'

Kaylee thoughtfully sipped her coffee. 'We've got two options that I can see. First is to see if Hadley can help; failing him, we can try Lex. Second, see if Patrick, aka Feral, can help. I don't really want to bother the Carltons if I can avoid it. I mean, I *assume* Mr and Mrs Carlton don't have anything to do with Eric's actions. They looked like solid people, came off a farm, and I saw them when they'd heard of their son's accident. They were distraught. It would be cruel to add the chance their son is a kidnapper to their burden at this stage.'

✻ ✻ ✻

On a dusty road east of town, Elise plodded along, somewhat cheered by the fact she now had an objective for her walk. Her stomach still growled uncomfortably but her eyes were firmly fixed on the roof shining in the fitful sun. She fervently hoped the building she could see in the distance was inhabited. She allowed herself a small positive daydream. *They'll ring Mum. She'll come and get me. I can have a shower and some proper food. Oh, let there be people there!* But at the back of her mind was the harsh knowledge that she'd seen no signs of habitation in any of the paddocks she had passed and could not see any signs that the paddocks she was passing right now had been farmed in a long while. She kept glancing at the sky, noting that the clouds were thickening and beginning to look threatening. She felt somewhat discouraged about her progress without realising that because of her early start she had walked about ten kilometres.

CHAPTER 14

Karah thoroughly enjoyed the guided walk that morning. They had passed through towering eucalypts and abundant wildflowers, including the delicate chocolate lily and subalpine scrub. The ranger kept up an informative commentary the whole way. The highlight for Karah had been when he drew their attention to a magnificent wedge-tailed eagle soaring high on the thermal updraughts. It was all magical to Karah, but she reminded herself, as she ate a welcome lunch, that there was serious work ahead of them, observing a planned hazard reduction burn. She gently prompted Ava to take advantage of their break to eat because it might be a while before their next rest. The guide had detailed the allotted time for the burn but added that fires were always unpredictable and this one might go to plan and be over quickly or there might be some hiccups that would mean it took longer.

The guide continued his instructive address while the students rested on log seats and ate. The National Parks had limited resources for fighting fires, only one patrol vehicle with a pump on Mount Kaputar. Today, they had enlisted the assistance of the Rural Fire Service. While the ranger was talking, two fire service trucks rumbled into the clearing and pulled up. They were closely followed by a smaller patrol vehicle and the National Parks vehicle. At the sight of the sturdy trucks with their complicated collections of hoses, pumps, fittings and equipment, Karah finally realised the seriousness of the task ahead of the teams. She had a dim inkling that the presence of a group of inexperienced students would add a further layer of difficulty to the work of the firefighters. She knew the National Parks employees were paid, but it had been made very clear to the students that all Rural Fire Service crews were volunteers who had paid work of their own that was being neglected while they were fighting fires. She felt a rush of gratitude for these hardworking and dedicated people.

'Right, so you see this area of cleared space above where we are, along the side of the road, that's the firebreak,' the ranger continued. 'The fire won't jump that and the forest won't burn. We are going to burn right along this side of the ridge. Can't slash this long grass, the ground is too rough, too many rocks. The RFS trucks are set high off the ground to lessen the chances of damage from obstacles. We burn from the top down. The fire meets the updraught on the mountainside and slowly burns down the slope. We wait down there along the next scrub line and prevent the fire from entering that area. As you can see,' he gestured with a wide sweep of his arm, 'we have about five hundred metres of heathland across the side of the mountain to burn today.'

The ranger looked around the group. 'For lighting fires, matches are too short-lived and unreliable. We use these drip torches.' He held up what looked like a small watering can with a longish thin spout. 'They are filled with a mixture of about fifty-fifty diesel and petrol. Light the wick and it continues to burn steadily while the operator moves along the area to be ignited.'

He glanced at his watch. 'Once you have finished your lunch, I would like you all to move down the slope to the scrub line. You can follow the RFS vehicles down. They will be patrolling across the fire front between you and the fire, ensuring your safety. It is very important that you listen to, and follow, all instructions immediately. You need to bear in mind that these people are all highly trained and experienced whereas you are not. If a problem arises, your prompt response to any directions could mean the difference between life and death.'

Karah looked at Ava and shuddered.

The RFS vehicles growled into life and slowly set off down the slope. Five or six men stationed themselves, evenly spaced across the mountainside, along the ridge top at the edge of the fire break. Once the RFS vehicles had reached the lower scrub line, they, too, spaced themselves along the expected fire front. The students stayed below the firefighters but positioned themselves so they could see the action. Karah and Ava positioned themselves at the end of the group, a short distance from the nearest student and the RFS truck.

When everyone was in place, the ranger gave the signal to go. The firefighters along the fire break lit their drip torches and applied the burning tips to the dry combustible undergrowth.

Small tongues of fire began flickering across the mountainside, some burning brightly when they hit tussocks of dried grass, others creeping slowly down the hill. Smoke rose in fine tendrils, gradually thickening.

From her position down the slope, Karah found it a frightening sensation knowing a fire was burning towards her. Steadily the flames gained size and speed.

Suddenly an errant breeze blew up in the scrub below her. It danced and spiralled past her, zigzagging up the slope. The little breeze split around the scattered trees and grew quickly into several willy-willies carrying dust and dried grass and twigs. They crossed the approaching fire line, gathering burning sticks and leaves and spreading them wide. Each burning piece lit a fresh fire. With each new fire, the heat increased and caused the wind to blow more strongly. The fire took on a life of its own.

In no time, the burn-off area had gone from a sedately burning line to a chaotic collection of random fires being spread up and down the slope by the strengthening erratic wind. Fires were carried forward, close to the line of firefighters and students. More dangerously, some fires started up the rise beyond the firebreak. Thick smoke billowed and swirled. The fire was already much too big for the firefighting resources on the mountain.

Karah grabbed Ava's hand and they stood frozen in horror. A new blaze cracked into fierce hot flames metres in front of them. Ava turned and ran headlong downhill into the scrub.

'Wait, Ava! Come back, we've got to stay together.' Karah's frantic scream was drowned by the sound of the wind and snapping flames. Eucalyptus trees swayed wildly in the wind, dropping leaves and dead branches as fresh fuel for the fire. Karah turned and ran in the direction she had last seen her friend.

✳   ✳   ✳

On her lonely road, east of Muswellbrook, Elise kept putting one tired foot in front of the other. She wasn't sure whether it was the thought of someone being in the building she could see ahead that cheered her or the fact that her stomach had finally eased its painful protest. At last, she arrived at the top of the long driveway.

Her heart sank as she scanned the road beneath her feet. No vehicle had passed this way recently. All she could see was dust and gravel, crisscrossed by faint ant tracks and dotted by the odd raindrop. Her shoulders sagged in disappointment as she realised there would be no easy rescue. *Oh well, best go and see what the place has to offer. Hopefully at the very least a roof over my head.* This last thought was prompted by increasingly heavy drops of rain beginning to fall. She increased her pace and finally stumbled onto the front veranda of the house, noting the derelict air of the place and the unkempt garden.

Elise knocked without hope. No response came from anywhere. No barking dogs, no voice calling 'Coming!', no children yelling. She only heard the now steady drum of rain on the corrugated iron roof. She tried the handle of the door and gave a satisfied sigh when it opened. Inside, the house was as bare and deserted as the last one she'd been in. She went through to the kitchen, carefully standing her water bottles on the bench and laying her little stock of food beside them. She tried the tap. Clear cold water ran into the sink. *Thank goodness! Big 'Yay!' for farmers and their rainwater tanks.*

Unencumbered by her belongings, Elise began a thorough exploration. Opening what she assumed had been the linen cupboard, she discovered a folded floral sheet and an old landline telephone. *The sheet could be handy. Wonder if the landline is still connected. Faint hope, I guess but I have to try everything.*

She carried the telephone with her, searching for the wall socket; she found it low down near the floor in what must have been the living room. She set the phone on the floor with the handset resting in the cradle and pushed the plug into the socket. Holding her breath, she lifted the handset to her ear. Silence! *Dammit, when am I going to get a break?*

She left the useless phone on the floor and went to investigate the bathroom. *Oh, Eureka! Bliss!* The departing residents had left a small sliver of soap in the dish of the shower stall, and even more exciting, Elise discovered half a roll of toilet paper. She knew she would savour a soapy shower, even though it would be a cold one and what luxury to be able to use toilet paper! She wanted to wash her clothes as well.

She listened to the falling rain and decided exploring the garden could wait. Using her fast-developing ingenuity, Elise tore the sheet in half. She enjoyed a long shower, washed her hair, and stood enjoying the feeling of fresh clean skin until the cold water cooled her too much. She used half the sheet as a towel and afterwards wrapped the other half round herself like a sarong. She wrapped her washed clothes in the damp sheet and twisted it into a sausage, turning tight to wring out the excess water. She hung her sheet/towel on one towel rail and draped her clothes on the other to dry. She opened the window to let in the little breeze that accompanied the rain.

Elise felt like a new person after the shower. She risked a look at herself in the mirror. Her reflection showed grey bags under her eyes. She raked her fingers through her hair, tidying it back off her face. *I haven't lost any weight, though.*

Then she laughed out loud. *It's only been two days, you galah. How much weight did you expect to lose in that time?*

The rain dwindled and she noted the daylight was beginning to fade. In the back garden, she discovered much the same as the last place in the way of past-their-best vegetables and the addition of a walnut tree weighed down with a bumper crop of nuts. She was astonished to find an apricot tree, netted to keep off the birds, with round plump fruit on every branch.

She pulled up a carrot and an onion. She grabbed a double handful of walnuts and holding her sarong up to make a basket, she carried them to the apricot tree. She couldn't resist devouring a couple of the juicy fruits straight away. She added a few to her haul and took the lot inside. Dumping it all on the bench, she went outside for one last item: half a brick she'd seen by the back door. She carefully washed everything, including the brick.

Elise used the brick to crack open a handful of walnuts, then she used it to mash the nuts, onion and carrot. Lastly, she mashed two apricots into the mess to sweeten it all. Scraping it into a pile, she ate her exotic 'dinner' with her fingers. *Actually, not bad. The walnuts gave it all a bit of substance.* She grinned at the thought of telling Diego about this meal. Even with his famous disdain for spending time on cooking, this would surely open his eyes.

❊ ❊ ❊

West of town, Graham Buckley glanced at the sky. Years of experience told him that while it was most likely raining east of town, the rain was unlikely to extend this far west. 'Jan,' he called. 'I'm just going down to Burt's. I promised him that copy of *The Landholder* with the article about market gardens. Shouldn't be long.'

'Fine, love. Say hi to Gisella for me. We'll have to all get together for a barbie soon.'

'I agree. Give us a kiss and I'll see you shortly.'

Jan waved casually as he left.

CHAPTER 15

Driving between the lion-topped pillars of Croham, Graham frowned. He saw two cars drawn up at the front of the house. He recognised Silvio's car but looked hard at the other car, a silver BMW. *That looks like the car that was outside my place this morning with the bloke crawling on the logs.*

'Come in, come in,' Gisella called, welcoming him when he knocked.

'How are you, Gisella?' He kissed her cheek. 'Jan sends love, says we'll get together for a meal soon.'

'Lovely, lovely. We might have bit more time on our hands. Burt hired young man to give us a hand with garden while his arm in plaster. Come through, Burt and Silvio in sunroom.'

Graham followed Gisella in her customary colourful swirling caftan through the house. In the sunroom, a chubby baby crawled after a toy on the rug. Burt was seated and Silvio was standing talking to a man who was a stranger to Graham but who looked familiar. Graham frowned again. Seeing the man as well as the car out the front, he was sure it was the same bloke he'd seen climbing on the logs that morning.

Introductions were made and Graham filed away the

name Trevor Laverty. It rang no bells, but he was suspicious. Burt was cheerful, pleased at the prospect of an extra pair of hands, and conversation flowed easily. Trevor seemed quiet, more content to watch than to contribute to the conversation. Graham sensed that Silvio had some reservations about Trevor, too. But then he remembered Silvio had a young baby and mentally shrugged, thinking Silvio could just as easily be tired as suspicious.

'So, Trevor. How did you hear about the job here?' Graham figured a little probing mightn't hurt.

'I saw the ad on the notice board at the shop.'

'What were you doing way out here? We're not exactly on the beaten track.'

'Oh, just driving around. I finished a job up Tamworth way and wanted a bit more work before I went on to Sydney.' Tobias had his heart in his mouth. He still didn't have much made up in the way of a backstory, hadn't had time. Burt had put him to work, all the time giving endless instructions.

'You got family in Sydney?' Graham was carefully watching Trevor/Tobias and had the feeling he was uneasy to be answering too many questions.

'Nah, I come from up north.'

Not giving much away, this young fella, Graham thought.

Silvio spoke to Tobias, 'You'd better get going up to the stud, Trevor, so you can get settled and washed up for dinner. Mrs Sullivan dishes up at six-thirty.'

'Right, I'll be off then. See you tomorrow, Mr Bunrack.'

Burt waved as Tobias left.

'Yeah well, I just dropped in with this magazine for you, Burt. Jan will have dinner ready soon, so I guess I'd better not stay long. Glad you've got someone to give you a hand. That'll let the pressure off you, eh Silvio?'

'Sure will, Graham. Mama is always happy to have Oliver but even so, there never seems to be enough hours in a day.'

'Oh, Silvio, I just remember,' Gisella cut in hurriedly. 'I not tell you and this for you too, Graham! Sharon call me yesterday. Terrible news. Elise has been kidnapped!'

'Good grief, Ma! How could you forget to tell me that?'

'Oh, that's terrible. Poor Bill and Sharon!' Graham spoke with genuine feeling. He was well acquainted with his daughter-in-law's extended family.

'Yes, Sharon very upset. Burt and me, we very anxious for them. I said come out on the weekend. She think about it. If they come, I ring Jan and you two come down. We have lunch. Cheer them up. Silvio, *caro*, you come too. You and Susannah.'

'Ma, how come it's not on the news? Don't they always call for public help? You know, "Has anyone seen? ... blah blah," and put up a picture.'

'I ask Sharon that. She say not good for Elise business when she get back. How can you be private investigator and not be private?' They all quietly put the emphasis on Elise being found and her life returning to normal.

'Oh, right. Got you. Terrible job, really. She should do something else.' Silvio made no secret of his distaste for Elise's career choice.

'I'll tell Jan. Heck, talking of Jan, I'd best get a move on! We'd love to join you if you're having a get-together, thanks, Gisella. Let us know and Jan will fix a plate of something to bring. Bye Burt, look after that arm. Bye, Gisella.'

'I'll walk out with you. Better get home to Zannah. See you tomorrow, Dad.' Silvio waved to his father and kissed his mother's cheek.

'My boy,' she said softly, stroking his arm.

'You sure you're okay to have Oliver for the night, Ma?'

'Pfft. No trouble at all. He's a beautiful, good boy aren't you, *caro*?' She squeezed the baby contentedly. 'Me and Papa love having him, don't we?'

'Yeah, 'e's no trouble. Thanks, Graham. See ya. I won't come out. Feelin' me age today.'

'Goodbye all.' Graham waved and followed Silvio.

Before he got in his car, he said quietly to Silvio, 'What do you reckon about that Trevor guy?'

Silvio glanced back towards the house, making sure his mother hadn't followed them outside. 'He seems a bit dodgy, doesn't have a lot to say for himself. No references. Can't even give the name of the last fella who hired him. He's not a worker. Did you see his hands? Too soft. And he hasn't got any boots. I asked Mac to let him stay in the workers' cottage at the stud, rather than having him stay in the house with my folks.'

'Good idea. Well, Silvio, I have to tell you this even though it might be nothing. But I thought I saw him on my place this morning, crawling over those logs I've got piled up to burn in my front paddock.'

Silvio stared. 'What would he do that for?'

'I dunno. Been wondering that myself. When I drove down there, he lit out bloody fast. I'm sure it's the same car, but of course I didn't note the number plate.'

'Weird. Well, if you have doubts and I have doubts, I'm not happy having him working here at Ma and Dad's without doing some checking. It's too late in the day now, but I'll ring Kaylee or Ben in the morning and see what they say. You remember Kaylee and Ben, don't you? The two detectives who helped us when Susannah's mum was killed. I'm going to ask them why it's taking them so long to find Elise, too. What shocking news that was.'

Graham nodded. 'Yeah, Jan'll be upset about that. You get on to the police. And Silvio, do a better job than me and get the number plate to them! They'll be able to get you some background, surely.'

'Yep. Thanks, Graham. Let's just keep our worries to ourselves for now. I'll let you know if I find out anything.'

'Right-oh, talk to you soon.'

Graham shared the gist of that conversation with Jan

when he got home. Of course, Jan was distressed on her daughter-in-law's behalf when he told her Elise was missing. Like Graham, she liked the family, knew them well. They discussed that news while they ate. They also went over Graham seeing the mysterious man on the log piles, puzzled but unable to come up with any answers that made sense.

'Well, love. Silvio will check with the police about this Trevor guy, and he'll be sure to let you know what he discovers,' Jan said as she cleared away the dishes.

* * *

Evander, Damien and Christos were dealt with harshly at the police station. The police wanted to arrest all three of them and lock them up on charges of car theft. The police officers took it as a personal affront that cars were being rebirthed almost in front of their eyes. The garage was closed, locked and everything in it was sealed behind police tape. Damien was deeply shocked that his easy line of income had proven so very vulnerable. One tiny thing like his father hiring that woman investigator had led to her disappearance and then to intense questioning by the police. That in turn had led to the discovery of his car rebirthing business. Christos, being less involved in the administration side of the business, was more naïve about how rebirthing cars equated with dealing in stolen cars. He was bewildered by the speed at which everything had changed. He had never expected to end up in jail.

Evander was aghast at the turn of events. His life was rapidly becoming a tangled mess and he dated that downturn to the day he hired Elise Dean. It was slowly becoming clear to him that Rhea had the better attitude when it came to the feud between the Nesters and the Lardners. He bitterly regretted hiring a private detective to investigate the Lardner lad. With difficulty, he acknowledged what a foolish mistake it was to think he was entitled to interfere in his daughter's life. The dismal state of his marriage had been weighing heavily on his mind. He missed having Rhea to turn to and discuss problems with and had been slowly reaching the decision to work hard at reviving their previous closeness. He hoped it wasn't too late.

Alone in the holding cell at the police station, Evander made a sudden harsh decision. He decided to leave his sons to look after themselves. He asked for and was given permission to make a call and rang his solicitor. He strenuously pursued the argument that he had his own business and wasn't involved in the running of the garage. He said he had simply called on his sons to discuss family issues and was unfortunately at his sons' place of business when the police arrived. The solicitor presented a fair case in support of Evander's claims, and with extreme reluctance, the police released him with a court attendance notice. He was ordered to report to the police station the next day for further questioning and was warned of the consequences if he was foolish enough to try to leave the district. He formally engaged the solicitor to act on Damien's and Christos' behalf, asking him to try for a bail hearing as soon as possible. He assured the solicitor he was willing and able to meet the security requirement for his sons' bail. He left the police station with mixed feelings. On the one hand, he was deeply sorry to be abandoning his sons, but he felt he had done all he could for them. On the other hand, although relieved to be going home, he was dreading explaining this latest fiasco to Rhea.

* * *

Rhea arrived home from her day in Newcastle tired but happy. She always enjoyed her outings with Cleo. Her light-hearted mood quickly turned to dismay when she saw Evander was already home and appeared to be in a mood as black as thunder. Millie was on the lounge beside him and he was absent-mindedly stroking her head. He already had a drink in his hand, and she briefly wondered if it wasn't the first.

'Hi, love. Thanks for letting Millie in. What's the matter, dear? You look awfully upset.'

Evander knew only too well that none of his current difficulties were Rhea's fault and tried to let go of his anger. He was conscious that if he ripped up at her, it certainly wouldn't help their marriage. His resolve to work on his marriage strengthened. If he couldn't fix his marriage, he didn't know how he would carry on. He had already let it slide badly. He squared his shoulders and breathed out his anger.

'Nothing for you to worry about, love. Go get yourself a drink and come and tell me about your day.'

Rhea was pleasantly surprised by his inviting tone of voice and happily went into the kitchen. He heard her put a glass on the bench, heard her phone ringing. He could hear her voice but not her words and then she screamed. He heard the glass smash on the floor. She screamed again. Heart in his mouth, Evander strode into the kitchen. Rhea was holding the phone rigidly to her ear, white-faced, eyes wide. He snatched the phone.

'Who's this?' he growled.

'Er, this is Pelle. Who is this please?'

'Evander Nester. What have you said to my wife?'

'I lecture at the university. I took your daughter and her student group to Mount Kaputar on an excursion and now Karah and her friend, Ava, are missing.'

'WHAT?' Evander put his free arm around Rhea and half dragged, half carried her to the couch. He sat beside her with his arm around her shoulder. Millie, sensing trouble, pressed close to Rhea's other side. Evander put the phone on speaker.

'Explain to me. Where is Mount Kaputar?' he said curtly.

'I was offered the chance for the students to observe a controlled hazard reduction burn in the Mount Kaputar National Park. It's a bit over three hours northwest of Muswellbrook at Narrabri. The fire got out of control.'

'Oh, God! Go on.' Evander rubbed his hand across his face, feeling his heart racing with anxiety.

'The students were spread out across the mountainside. There was smoke and flames everywhere.'

'Karah, what about Karah?'

'She and Ava are missing. They got separated from the group. Two students and a volunteer firefighter are in hospital in Narrabri with minor injuries. I've sent the bus home with the rest of the students. But I'll stay here. They're still fighting the blaze, as well as searching for the girls.'

'Oh, God, what can I do?'

'Well, nothing, Mr Nester. There's no phone signal on the mountain. So, you can't try calling Karah. I am very sorry, but there is nothing you can do. I will keep you updated but the situation on the mountainside is very dangerous and chaotic.'

'You ring this number IMMEDIATELY when you have some news. Immediately! I don't care what time it is, ring me!'

Evander laid down the phone and pulled his wife into his embrace. Against his chest, he felt her deep sobs shudder through her body.

'Oh, my little baby! All by herself in a fire on a mountain. Evander, what can we do?'

'Nothing, love. Nothing. We just have to wait and hope. Oh, poor little Karah.' His voice broke.

CHAPTER 16

'Hey, Feral, it's Tobias. How's Snake?'

Tobias had been jittery ever since Graham had been at the Bunrack's farm asking questions. He was sure it was the guy who had chased him off the log piles. He HAD to find that private investigator. Time was getting short. All night his mind had been going backwards and forwards between trying to forget about the investigator and needing to find her. He'd woken early and abruptly decided to locate her.

'Ahh, no change.' *Why the devil is bloody Tobias ringing at this hour of the morning?*

'Look, man, you know I wouldn't bother you if it wasn't urgent, but where would Snake hide a girl he'd kidnapped?'

'What?'

Tobias repeated the question and added a brief explanation. 'He didn't tell me where he was taking her but now, I have to find her.'

'Jeez, Tobias. Are you nuts? How the hell would I know where he'd hide her? What sort of a shit mate are you, dragging him into your stupid scheme?'

'You'd better have a little think, mate.' Tobias resented the implication of his careless disregard for his friend, mainly because he knew it was true. His voice hardened. 'You don't want your brother charged with murder, do you? She might be starving to death right now.'

'Bloody hell!' Feral thought a bit. 'I suppose you could try the farm where we grew up, out on Bees Hive Road,' Feral said reluctantly. He didn't want to get his brother in trouble, but he didn't like the thought of a woman possibly dying. He was a wild lad but not a cruel one and he still had some sense of chivalry.

'What number?' Tobias snapped.

'5750. It's a chance he hid her there. But he might not have. He's never liked being out in the country.'

'Well, you'd better hope you're right.' Tobias hung up without a word of thanks, leaving Patrick feeling confused and resentful.

Sod this, I'm going to find her. I don't need this bloody gardening job. Quickly, Tobias flung his things into his bag and threw it in his car. Trying not to rev the engine too loudly and draw attention to his departure, Tobias drove away up the dusty road towards Wheeler, happily leaving behind his short-lived job as a gardener.

*   *   *

In the early grey morning light, Evander let Millie out the back for a quick run and brewed himself a coffee. He hadn't slept. Rhea's anguish pierced him. He had never felt so powerless. His daughter missing in a bushfire and his sons in jail. *What a disaster!* Eventually he had given Rhea a sedative to calm her distraught tears and she was deeply asleep now.

His mind churned over all the things he had learned in the past twenty-four hours. Gradually his focus zeroed in on Tobias Lardner. His thoughts swirled around, a mixture of hatred, futile worry, despair and impotent fury. *That little bastard has organised Eric Carlton to snatch that private investigator. God, I wish I'd never gone near her. She could be in real trouble if Eric is the only one who knows where she is. It'll be murder if she dies. Otherwise, why would the cops be questioning all of us? Where the hell has Eric dumped her? Where?* He racked his brains. *Oh, I know! Perfect! His dad's abandoned farm! Their farm was out east, wasn't it? All those farms out there have been empty since the mines bought them all up. The perfect place. If I can get out there and rescue her, I'll have some leverage with the cops and Rhea will be impressed as well. Now, where exactly was their farm? Bees Hive Road? Yes. That's it! I went out there once to pick Snake up for something. Must have been when he first started working in the garage.*

Without further thought, he quickly let the dog back in and quietly dressed. As he left the bedroom, Millie jumped on the bed and snuggled close to Rhea's sleeping body. Evander drove east through the early morning mist shrouding the slowly waking town.

❊　❊　❊

'Good morning, Ben. What a great day after that little shower of rain yesterday.'

'Morning, boss.' Ben got straight down to work. 'I've been onto Hadley and Lex Lardner and neither of them seem to have any idea where Tobias is. I'm afraid we'll have to disturb the Carltons and talk to Patrick. Can't hold up the search for Elise any longer.'

'Okay, Ben. Call him.'

❊　❊　❊

Standing anxiously by his brother's bedside, Patrick was trying to take in what the doctor was saying as well as support his mother who seemed in danger of collapse. His phone rang, again. Smothering an exasperated sigh, he gently lowered his mother into a chair and, frowning, took his phone out into the corridor.

'Patrick, this is Detective Senior Constable Ben Wharton. I'm very sorry to disturb you. How is your brother doing?'

'Ahh, no change.' *What now?* Patrick stifled his impatience.

'Sorry to hear that. I won't keep you long.' Ben sucked in

his breath as a sudden brainwave hit him and he changed his question. 'Ah, can you tell me the address of the farm your parents had before they retired?'

Patrick's voice changed from mystified to enlightened. *Huh, that bastard, Tobias, thinks he can threaten me with that woman dying. I'll fix him! This sounds like the cops are onto him and I bloody hope they are. I hope they've realised she could be at Dad's old place.* Little realising he was implicating his brother as well as Tobias, he quickly answered in a hard voice. 'Sure. Their place was 5750 Bees Hive Road.'

'Oh, that's great. Thank you so much.' Ben disconnected the call. 'Yahoo, boss!' He punched the air. 'Yours truly, the genius strikes again!'

'What are you on about, Ben?'

'I didn't have to question Patrick at all. I just remembered you saying the Carltons had a farm and I wondered if Eric had dumped Elise in the bush somewhere there. Patrick tells me their farm was out east where the coal mines bought up all those farms. Heaps of empty farmhouses out there. All we have to do is search them, starting with the Carlton place.'

Kaylee looked admiringly at Ben. 'Wow, Benny-boy. You've done it again! Great stuff. What are we still doing here?'

✻   ✻   ✻

Tobias drove wildly through Wheeler and on into town, forgetting his resolve to obey speed limits and be a law-abiding citizen. Now that he had decided on a course of action, he wanted to waste no time. He was relieved when the familiar streets of town changed the scenery. Barely slowing, he skirted around the main streets; searching for the road he wanted had him huffing with impatience. His search was hindered by the thinning morning mist. Then he found Bees Hive Road and once again pressed his foot hard on the accelerator. The countryside streamed past, trees and paddocks, but there was no traffic to slow him down. After a while, the bitumen was replaced by unsealed road. This gradually deteriorated to a rutted and pot-holed track. Tobias was driving far too fast for the conditions and several times skidded dangerously on corners.

At one point, he overcorrected from a skid, sending the car careering backwards off the road. *Jeez!* The sudden stop jerked his head savagely. The engine stalled and Tobias had to take a moment to gather his wits. *That was close!* Fortunately, he hadn't hit any trees or hidden boulders on the edge of the road. After a little manoeuvring, he managed to get his car back on the road. Once back on the road, he drove a few metres, very slowly, listening for sounds of anything amiss with the car. Reassured that everything sounded normal, he carried on a little more sedately while his heart rate returned to normal. He started to look for numbers on mailboxes. The numbers represented, not the lot number of the property, but the distance from the post office in town. This system had been introduced to make it easier for emergency services such as police, ambulance and fire departments to locate addresses in times of trouble. Thus, 5750 Bees Hive Road was 57.5 kilometres from the post office.

Tobias almost missed the driveway. The long grass partly obscured the bleached old mailbox, and the number was faded, nearly indecipherable. He swung the car in and bumped down the short, curved driveway. He looked around curiously. Snake had never talked much about his life on the farm. Tobias took in the weatherboard house and tried to imagine how it must have looked when Snake and his family lived there. It looked very rundown now. He switched off the car and listened through the open window to the ticking as the engine cooled. Apart from that faint sound and the carolling of magpies, all was quiet. He squared his shoulders and stepped from the car. *Here goes nothing. I hope she's in here.*

Stepping up to the door, Tobias noted that it was slightly ajar. He listened for a moment, heard no sound from inside. He gently pushed the door. It seemed stuck on something, so he gave it a sharp shove. He paused for a moment and in that instant, Elise's carefully laid ambush of stones in the old cast-iron pot above the door smashed down on him. Tobias collapsed face down, full length on the floor, deeply unconscious, bleeding from the gash the pot had left on his head.

*   *   *

As he drove along Bees Hive Road, Evander noted remembered landmarks. *The bitumen should end soon. Ahh, yep. Just here. Better ease off the speed a bit.*

He was reluctant to slow down too much because, like Tobias, now he had decided on a course of action, he was impatient to get it done. Unlike Tobias, though, he realised the need for caution on such a rough road. Suddenly, he spotted the shabby mailbox beside the sagging gate and drove carefully in between the weathered posts. Coming within sight of the rusty corrugated iron roof and the weatherboards of the homestead, Evander was shocked to see a car in the driveway. Switching off the engine, he warily stepped out of his car. He trod quietly around the back of the other car as he approached the veranda, eyes darting suspiciously left and right.

The sight of two feet on the floor in the doorway made his blood run cold. He froze and listened. Hearing nothing other than the peaceful sounds of the bush, he crept closer. He quickly glanced behind himself to be sure he was alone, then inched towards the door.

Stretched out on the floor, Tobias remained unmoving.

Evander watched the inert man for a few moments, noting the slight but steady motion of the rib cage, up and down in time with the slow breathing. He took in the cast-iron pot and the bleeding gash. *Who the hell is this? Where is the girl? What's happened here?*

✻   ✻   ✻

As the last of the morning mist rose, Ben drove out of town along Bees Hive Road.

'Seems a waste for all this good farmland to be doing nothing while waiting for coal field expansion,' he commented.

Kaylee nodded, looking around at the empty paddocks and straggling grass. Her phone rang. 'Hello? This is Detective Sergeant Kaylee Bradshaw.'

'Kaylee! It's Silvio Bunrack.'

'Silvio. How lovely to hear from you. How's fatherhood treating you?' Despite the many difficulties of the police investigation into Silvio's mother-in-law's murder, Kaylee maintained a warm and genuine friendship with Silvio and his wife, Susannah.

'Love it, Kaylee, you've no idea! But look, I don't want to hold you up and I've got a problem.'

'Shoot, Silvio. Always glad to help.'

Silvio detailed his father's accident and the hiring of an extra hand. 'The thing is, both Graham Buckley and I have

171

reservations about this guy, Trevor Laverty.' Silvio detailed his worries and added Graham's observations, finishing with, 'Have you got anything on him? I can give you his car rego.'

'Fire away, Silvio. I'll check and get straight back to you. Sorry to hear Burt's laid up.'

'Cheers, Kaylee. Thanks, appreciate it.'

Kaylee closed the call and keyed the registration details into the laptop fitted in the police vehicle.

'Oh my god! Ben, listen to this. Silvio's dad has hired Tobias Lardner to help in his market garden! Tobias is using the name of Trevor Laverty. Silvio was suspicious of him having no references and a flimsy backstory. So now we know where Tobias is!'

Quickly, Kaylee rang Silvio back with the details. She explained that the police wanted Tobias in connection with the disappearance of a female private investigator.

'Oh, God, no! Not Elise! Ma just told us yesterday that she's missing.'

'How do you know her? And how did you know about it?'

'She's my cousin. My dad and her mum are brother and sister. The family shared.'

'Oh dear, I'm so sorry. We're right now pursuing a strong lead in hopes of locating poor Elise, so we can't get out to you straight away. Tobias is not considered dangerous. Just thoughtless and impulsive. You'd be doing us an enormous favour if you keep an eye on him, so he doesn't disappear again while we're out following up this lead on Elise.'

'So long as he doesn't pose a threat to my family. Mama's got baby Oliver with her and Dad's pretty useless with his arm in plaster.'

'At any sign of trouble, call the station. Talk to you soon.' Kaylee disconnected. She turned to Ben. 'We'll go straight out there and grab that slippery little Tobias after we search this place for Elise.'

'Right, boss.' Ben kept his eyes carefully on the winding way and slowed his speed to cope with the deteriorating road conditions.

❊   ❊   ❊

Evander's confused thoughts were interrupted by the unexpected sound of an approaching vehicle. He whirled and felt his heart start to hammer. A police car was slowing to a halt behind his car.

'Well, well, well, what have we here, Ben?'

The two police officers carefully exited their car. From his side, closer to the house, Ben could see Evander standing on the veranda.

'Evander,' he called, 'don't do anything silly. Just walk slowly to me with your arms out.'

Evander? Kaylee's mind was spinning. *Who else is here?* She prudently scanned her surroundings, checking for hidden dangers in the form of possible other people.

She heard Ben speak again. 'Is anyone with you, Evander?'

'There's a bloke unconscious in the doorway. But I haven't seen anyone else.'

Evander stopped a few feet in front of Ben, and Kaylee walked around the police car to join him. 'You'd better tell us what's going on.'

'I think you need an ambulance. That guy is out cold.'

'Stay here,' Kaylee ordered.

With all her senses twitching, she approached the door with Tobias' two inert feet still sticking out. Stepping around him, she quickly scanned the room and then knelt and felt his neck for a pulse, noting the gash on his head.

'Ben!' she called. 'Cuff Evander to the car. Bring the first-aid kit and radio for an ambulance, once you've got Evander immobilised.'

'Evander ...' Ben looked steadily at the man. 'You know this has all the look of a very serious situation on top of the trouble you're already in. An unexplained injured man. Please don't do anything stupid. Your co-operation right now will be noted, I promise. Just quietly let me cuff you to the car. Did you come out here alone? Did you injure that guy? Who is he?'

'I'm on my own. I don't know who he is. I never touched him. I swear I got here just moments before you. He was laid out like a rug. Please believe me.'

Ben handcuffed Evander to the door handle of the back

passenger side door. 'All right, we'll carry this on later. Just wait here patiently and for your own sake don't do anything stupid.'

As he carried the first-aid kit to Kaylee, Ben radioed for the ambulance and a backup car.

Kaylee had moved Tobias into the recovery position by the time Ben stepped through the door.

'Hey, boss! That's Tobias Lardner! I know him. I interviewed him!'

Kaylee sat back on her heels and stared at Ben. Then she quickly began applying pressure to Tobias' bleeding head. 'Let Silvio know his worker has done a bunk, will you, Ben?'

'Right, boss.' While he dialled and spoke to Silvio, Ben prowled cautiously through the house. He checked out the bedrooms and the bathroom and entered the kitchen just as he finished his call to Silvio. *I knew it!* With a crow of victory, Ben pounced on the blue suede stiletto on the kitchen bench where Elise had left it.

'Look at this, boss! Elise has been here! I recognise that shoe. She could very well be here still. I'm going searching, if you're okay with the situation here?'

'By all means, go, look, and good luck. I'm fine here.'

Bemused, Silvio stared at his phone. The three short-spaced conversations with the police had left him stunned. This guy they'd hired to work for his dad was a suspect in Elise's disappearance! And now the guy had turned up with his head split open. *Good grief!* He was gratified that his suspicions had been correct and very glad he had acted on them. Even more glad that whatever had happened to the guy had happened far away from his family. He truly hoped the police would soon locate Elise. But now, of course, his father was shorthanded again.

He and Susannah had been about to drive to Croham to pick up Oliver. Silvio hurried Susannah into the car. He was anxious to get to his parents' and share all this news with them.

'What, Sil? What is going on? Tell me!' Susannah felt his impatience.

'I can't believe it, Zannah. I'm so shocked!'

'Sil! Share with me!' she demanded.

'We'll be at Ma and Dad's in a moment. I'll tell you all at the same time.'

Susannah huffed but sat quietly during the short drive to Croham. She was deeply grateful that the home they rented was on the farm next door to Silvio's parents. She wouldn't have to be in suspense for long. She liked the arrangement because Gisella was always so willing to have baby Oliver when she and Silvio had work commitments. She liked both her in-laws, got on well with them, had known them all her life. She realised she was very lucky to be in such a flexible workplace with a readymade babysitter on hand any time. Not that she was short of babysitters. Mrs Sullivan, who cooked for the workers at the stud, adored little Oliver. Her stepbrother and his wife were always happy to mind him as well.

* * *

Handcuffed to the police car, Evander felt his phone vibrate with an incoming call. *Oh God! That'll be Rhea. Oh, bloody hell, I didn't even leave her a note. What if they've found Karah? What if it's bad news? Oh, why have I been such a fool?*

* * *

Rhea felt sick. Her head ached from the combination of crying, lack of sleep, dehydration, lack of food and the sedative Evander had given her. She rolled over in bed and her hand felt Millie's soft fur. *Where was Evander? Had he received news of Karah?* Rhea picked up her phone and rang his number. It rang and rang and finally went to message bank. *Why wasn't he answering his phone?* Rhea felt lonely and confused. In serious need of an understanding friend, she rang Cleo.

CHAPTER 17

Elise woke early, feeling refreshed despite sleeping on the hard lino floor. She listened to the birds for a while, then made her way out to the garden for a breakfast of apricots.

As she enjoyed the juicy apricots, she took inventory of things she would need to do to ready herself once again for her trek. She screwed up her face when she realised the wet grass would be unsuitable to stuff her 'shoes'. *Maybe I should spend a day here, regrouping. I can scout through these sheds and see what I can find that might be useful. There might be some bags I can use for shoes. What I'd really love to do would be to find some matches and a pot of some kind and cook some vegetables. But that's just an idle dream. I'll see what I can find and then decide either to continue on my way or spend the day here. Probably should keep walking but my feet are too soft to last if I have nothing to stuff my shoes with. Wait! What's that? It's a vehicle! Is it Van Man coming back for me? Oh God! Where can I hide?*

Panic made her forget that she was quite a safe distance (roughly seventeen kilometres) from the house where Van

Man had dumped her. Quickly, she ran into the house. The driveway from the road was a long one and she knew she wouldn't be able to see any car that went along the road. She had barely been able to see this place from the road yesterday. Logic told her she would be very hard to spot from the road. She figured that her current position was reasonably safe but wanted a bolt hole in case someone came down that long driveway. *Hey! Is that another car? Too soon for Van Man to be coming back. Wish I could see the road. WHAT? Another car! Do I hide or run up to the road and flag them down? Too late. They've passed now.*

Elise hadn't envisioned having such a dilemma. She had only imagined Van Man coming back and her need to hide from him. She was dismayed to discover her heightened sense of vulnerability. She hadn't realised the toll her ordeal was taking on her. She wondered if the three cars were connected to Van Man or something entirely separate. She realised it was important to find somewhere she could hide but from where she could observe anyone coming to this house. Briefly, she allowed herself to imagine a police car arriving to rescue her. Then she gave herself a mental shake and began to think in practical terms of how to hide, how to see but remain unseen. *The roof! If anyone comes and I'm hiding on the roof, I can hide quietly behind the chimney. If I take up an armful of rocks, I can throw them on anyone who discovers me.*

Elise quickly swapped her curtain sarong for her own

clothes, which were much more suitable for climbing trees and roofs. The things she'd washed the evening before were mostly dry. She darted out the back door and ran to the shed to try and find a bucket or other container to carry her ammunition onto the roof. After a rapid search, she found some old bags. *Can stuff my shoes with these, too.* Shaking them out, she selected the strongest-looking one. Then she shoved several broken bricks into it, being careful not to make it too heavy. *Oh, now wait a moment. Really? Am I going to spend all day on the roof? That's stupid. It'll get hot up there. I'll get thirsty. I know! I'll get the bricks up there. Try to find a plastic bottle with a lid for water, better than glass ones with no lid, and put that up there. Then I'll work out the quickest way up onto the roof and wait on the ground until someone actually comes.*

Elise was too close to the problem to realise how scatterbrained her plans were. She failed to recognise the full extent of the impact of her ordeal, how much her fear was influencing her thinking, in fact, her whole mental state. Satisfied with this, to her, saner approach to her problem, Elise went in search of a plastic bottle with a lid. She found two and used the silt and water method to scour and clean them before filling them. Then she put them in the bag with the bricks and tied the neck of the bag with a length of the ubiquitous baler twine, easily found on most farms. Lugging the bag to the base of the walnut tree, she stepped back and tried to work out the best way to climb it. It was a big tree with spreading branches. One at about the same height as the gutter of the house seemed to offer the best hope. *Oh my! When did I last climb a tree?* Carefully swinging the bag over the lowest branch, Elise began to climb.

Without too much difficulty, she was soon slinging the bag of bricks onto the roof. She followed, making the transition from tree to roof without too much difficulty. She was just catching her breath when she heard another vehicle. She stepped swiftly up the roof, keeping the chimney between her and the driveway. Peering around, Elise was glad to find she had a good view of the road and the driveway. She was astonished to see an ambulance and a police car on the road heading away from town with lights flashing but no sirens. *Who would need an ambulance out there? I didn't think there WAS anyone out there!* Elise decided to wait for a while and see if there was any further activity.

❋   ❋   ❋

Karah was in agony. Her whole body hurt. She was sure her ankle was broken. It was swollen, the skin blue-black and stretched tight. Impossible to stand on. She was a lonely miserable mess, smudged with black ash, hair tangled by the scrub she had rushed through, bruises on every part of her body that had hit trees and rocks on her headlong flight away from the fire.

The previous afternoon, she and Ava had plunged recklessly down the mountainside, blinded by smoke, eyes streaming, their faces whipped by branches as they passed. Smoke and debris swirled around them, choking and disorienting them. When she paused in her flight to catch her breath, Karah looked around and couldn't see her friend anywhere.

'Ava. Ava! Stop. Wait for me. Stop!' No answer had come back to her. She could hear the roar of the fire, the growl of a firefighting truck and the shouts of the men as they fought the flames further up the slope. She lurched forward through the thick undergrowth. It was so steep that she was barely able to stay upright.

'A-vaaa!' Her call turned to a scream as she tripped on a fallen branch and rolled head over heels, bashing into rocks and branches. She stopped short against the trunk of a tree, dazed, her body hurting all over.

'Oh, Ava, where are you?' It came out as a tiny whimper.

She had tried to stand, but her ankle let her down and she fell, tumbling further down among the trees and undergrowth. She could hear flames crackling closer and the wind roaring in the treetops. She struggled upright, clinging to a sapling. Her ankle sent excruciating pain shooting up her leg and she toppled again. This time her plunge halted with her lying in a shallow gully. Her nostrils stung with smoke and wind-blown dirt and grit. She could feel the searing heat as the flames rushed nearer, almost upon her. *Oh, God!*

One last despairing plea. She curled up tight into a tiny ball, frightened beyond thought.

Karah cringed under the intense heat that suffocated her, sucking the oxygen from the air. She was deafened as the flames rushed over her, devouring all the dry material as they went. In seconds, the fire had burned past her, protected in her small hollow, leaving hot black ash all around her. Near hysteria, she lay sobbing with relief.

After a long, terrified night alone in the little depression, Karah lay listening to her surroundings. She had heard during the night, far away, the engines of vehicles, seen their flashing lights, seen the red fire glow. This morning, birdsong brightened the day, although the sky was still heavily smoke-smudged. Karah felt sickened by the overpowering stench of burnt scrub. Moving gingerly, she sat up and looked around. She was surprised to realise she still wore her backpack. She was very thirsty and quickly drank half her water bottle before realising that might be all the water she had for the foreseeable future. Recapping the bottle, she foraged in her pack and pulled out her phone. Her heart sank when she realised that she had no signal, disappointed tears spilling down her cheeks. She unearthed a snack bar left over from yesterday and ate it slowly.

It sounded like the fire might still be burning away to her left, but she couldn't tell accurately because she was so far down the slope. She had no clear idea where she was, her frightened flight down the mountainside was a blur.

'Ava, Ava!' she called. No answer came back. She felt alone in the blackened wasteland, dwarfed by the towering, charred tree trunks. Forlorn tears rolled down Karah's cheeks, leaving black streaks.

*　*　*

Ava rolled over groggily, her head was pounding. One eye seemed glued shut. She rubbed her hand over her face and realised her eye was stuck shut with dried blood.

'Karah?' her voice sounded small in the vastness of the national park. She rubbed her eye clear then looked around. She was stunned to see perfect natural bushland, unscarred at all by fire.

Ava gingerly stood up. She swayed dizzily and sat back down, slipping off her backpack and resting her back against a tree trunk. She was surprised and comforted that she hadn't lost her backpack in her mad flight down the mountainside. She fumbled through the contents, dragging out a banana and a half-filled water bottle. While she ate, she made an inventory of her body, relieved no bones seemed to be broken. She hardly felt bruised anywhere, to her surprise, but her head still throbbed. She ran her hand across her forehead and discovered a large bump that felt scabbed with dried blood. She pulled out her phone. No signal! She tried to remember the layout of the walks in Mount Kaputar but it was useless because she had no idea where she was. In the quiet of the bush, she heard the noise of a vehicle somewhere further down the slope.

Ava put her water bottle and phone back in her backpack and stood up.

❋   ❋   ❋

Cleo, brewing coffee in her kitchen, heard her phone vibrate on the bench. 'Hello?'

'Oh, Cleo.' Rhea's voice was high with tension. 'Karah's missing. Evander's missing. He gave me a sedative and I didn't hear him leave or anything. I can't get them on the phone. I'm so miserable. Can you come?' Her voice rose to a wail.

'Oh, my dear! How dreadful for you! I'll be over as soon as possible. Go and have a long hot shower while you wait for me. It'll make you feel better.'

Cleo quickly dressed, her mind spinning with questions. Rhea had sounded almost hysterical. As she drove across town to her friend's place, she rang Lex. 'Sweetheart, how are you?'

'Aw, Mum, not so good. Had a hell of a night. My girlfriend went on an excursion with her class, and they got caught in a fire. Karah and her friend, Ava, are missing.'

'I know. That's so awful. What a terrible worry for you, son.'

'What, Mum? How do you know Karah?'

Cleo smiled lovingly into the phone at his confusion. 'I know of her. Her mother and I are close friends except we only worked out yesterday that you two were dating.'

'You're lucky you got me. I'm on the road to Mount Kaputar and the phone reception is patchy.'

'What? You're on the road?'

'I couldn't sleep. Finally got up and left. I'm nearly there.'

'But what can you do?'

'Mum, I can either join the search or I can be with Karah when she's found. I have to think positively. She needs me. And I need to be with her.'

'Well, you take care, love. I'm just on my way over to Karah's mum's place now. She's beside herself with worry. Keep in touch with me, please. I'll be at Rhea's. I don't think she will be wanting to leave her house. She sounds like she had a pretty rough night as well.'

'I'll give you a call later, for sure. See how things are going for you and give you an update.'

Cleo disconnected after a fond goodbye as she drove into Rhea's driveway.

Rhea threw herself into her friend's arms, clinging to her and crying.

'Come inside, dear. I'm here for you. Come, sit on your lounge. Have you eaten? I'll get you a cup of tea.'

With Cleo calmly taking control, Rhea's feeble attempts to be rational and composed broke down completely. 'My baby girl lost in the scrub. Where is Evander? I can't stand this!' She sobbed wildly. Slumped down on the lounge, Millie pressed close to her, whining and licking her face.

❋　❋　❋

Damien and Christos left the police station and stood, bewildered, on the street. Their father's solicitor had worked hard and successfully argued for their bail. The police had told them that the garage was sealed and off-limits for them. Unfortunately, since they had both driven their cars to work yesterday, that meant their cars were unavailable to them as well.

'God, I'm hungry.' Damien finally spoke.

'Let's go downtown and have breakfast and we can work out what to do while we eat. I'm hanging out for a decent coffee.' Christos pulled out his phone and selected his father's name from the menu. He pressed 'call', then waited while it rang. In disgust, he disconnected when there was no answer. 'Where the hell do you think Dad's got to?' he grouched to his brother. 'He leaves us in the hands of the solicitor and now we're out, he can't be contacted.'

Damien was reluctant to think too badly of his father, but he had to agree with Christos that his father's actions puzzled him. 'Call a cab. We need a feed and some time to think through this whole mess.'

* * *

Evander, with both hands firmly locked around the door handle of the police car by the standard issue handcuffs, was frustrated when, yet again, his phone rang in his pocket. His mind ranged fearfully over all the people who could be calling him. Top of the list was Rhea, closely followed by his sons. He belatedly remembered that Karah's lecturer had called on Rhea's phone and most likely would not have his number. *But what if they found Karah and the lecturer rang Rhea? What if it was bad news? Rhea would be distraught, receiving bad news and not having him there to comfort her, not even knowing where he was.* His shoulders slumped and he dejectedly rested his forehead on the roof of the police car.

Inside the house, the ambulance officers were working to stabilise Tobias. He was semi-conscious and agitated, rambling incoherently. 'Where is she? What if she's dead? What if Snake dies?' The two ambulance officers looked at each other, mystified.

One of them said, 'Reckon his physical condition is just about stable now for the ride into hospital, don't you?'

'Yeah. His blood pressure is steady and the bleeding on his head has slowed. After such a knock on the head, he could be confused for a while. He'd certainly have a concussion.'

Kaylee, Ben and the two police officers from the backup car were methodically scouring the grounds of the farmhouse and the sheds, searching for Elise. Other than the lone blue suede stiletto, there was no sign she had been there. Ben and Kaylee returned to the front room of the house to see how the ambulance officers were progressing with Tobias.

'Kaylee.' The senior ambulance officer beckoned her. 'We've got this young man stable now and ready to be transported to hospital. You say he's known to you?'

'Yes, Adam. He is Tobias Lardner. Ben recognised him and I found his driver's licence in his wallet and other identifying cards. The first car in the line out the front is registered in his name. I'd say that's pretty conclusive. What would you say the prognosis is for him?'

'Oh, definitely concussion. They'll do x-rays at the hospital to check for broken bones, stitch that gash in his head. Overall, I'd say not life-threatening. Give me his wallet and phone. The hospital will contact his family.'

'Thanks, Adam. Great work. You right to get him out of here?'

'Yep. We'll manage. See you round, Kaylee.' With a smile and a wave, he turned to help his partner move Tobias onto the trolley.

Kaylee turned to her partner. 'Ben, do you reckon Evander was telling the truth about not harming Tobias? How did he get that injury?'

'Well, it looks to me as if the doorway was booby-trapped with that big pot balancing on top of the door and when

Tobias went in, it crashed down on him. A pretty clever idea, but a bit extreme. I reckon if I was a desperate, disoriented female kidnap victim, I might think of something like that.'

'And why do you say that?' The feminist in Kaylee made her reaction sharp and defensive.

'Cool it, cool it, boss. Think of it this way: a cornered or kidnapped bloke would be more likely to think of physical defence against his captors. We know from Elise's description she is slightly built. Unless she had martial arts training, which nobody has mentioned she has, she would be more likely to plan on using something other than her strength to combat her attacker.'

'Oh yes. I see what you're getting at. But wouldn't they have tied her up?'

'Hey, Ben. Take a look at this.' One of the searching police officers was stooping in the corner of the room. 'Looks like some short bits of duct tape.'

'Don't touch it!' Ben spoke sharply. 'Just bag it up for Forensics. Now, search for more duct tape or anything that could have been used to tie her hands or legs together. See, boss,' he turned excitedly to Kaylee, 'they must have taped her eyes or mouth or both! But she's managed to get the tape off. Maybe they DID tie her legs or arms, but she somehow got loose.'

'And she left. But where did she go and how? Did she booby-trap the door in case they came back?'

'Who would know? Let's see what Evander can add.'

* * *

Cleo was having trouble calming Rhea. The whining agitated dog added to the tension in the room. Distractedly she wondered if she should try to find the sedatives Evander had dosed Rhea with the night before and give her another one. She couldn't make sense of Evander's disappearance.

'Come on, sweetie. You MUST calm down. Everything possible is being done to find Karah, believe that. She's young and fit, she'll be fine.' Cleo's fingers were crossed behind her back, hoping she was speaking the truth. 'Drink your tea and I'll make you a nice warm muffin with marmalade.' Vaguely, Cleo recalled reading somewhere that sweet things were good for people suffering from shock and she was pretty sure Rhea was in shock. She handed Rhea a tissue. 'Come on, love. Take it easy. I'll be back in a jiffy.' She wrapped a throw rug around Rhea and the dog and went into the kitchen. She took the precaution of taking Rhea's phone from her and switching it to 'silent'. She thought Rhea was starting to settle down a bit and the last thing she wanted was to have a phone call setting her off again.

It was a sensible precaution. No sooner had she placed the phone on the bench than it began to vibrate with an incoming call. Cleo grabbed the phone and went out to the carport through the laundry, closing the door behind her so Rhea wouldn't hear.

'Hello?' The caller's identity had said Damien, so she knew it was Rhea's son. 'I'm your mother's friend, Cleo. She's a bit indisposed at the moment. Can I help you?'

'What's happened? Is Dad okay?' *Why is he asking about Evander?*

'Your mum hasn't been able to contact him. She's very upset because she and your dad heard last night your sister is missing in a bushfire. We're waiting for news but apparently your dad went somewhere this morning and isn't answering his phone.'

'What are you talking about? There are no fires round here.'

'She was on an excursion with her university class, somewhere north of here. Why did you ask about your dad? Is he okay?'

Damien quickly came to a decision. 'We're not sure where Dad is. But Christos and I will come straight around. Mum needs her family round her. We'll be there to support her and screen her calls. Can you wait there with her, er, Cleo, until we get there?'

CHAPTER 18

Ava had no idea how to travel using the sun as a guide. She had no clue how to orientate herself in terms of the points of the compass. She was a city girl in every way and her only known form of navigation was using the maps application on her phone. With no phone signal, she felt lost. She knew she only had a small reserve of water and food and had to find help fast. She simply figured that if she went downhill, she might come to some sign of habitation. Also, going downhill seemed easier than climbing back up. She was encouraged in her hopes for habitation by the occasional sounds of vehicles passing. She wondered where Karah was and whether she was okay.

* * *

At the Mount Kaputar carpark, a large group of volunteer fire-fighting personnel, National Park staff and State Emergency Service volunteers were gathered. Some were weary from fighting the fire during the night. Others were fresh, having been called in that morning to help with the search for the two missing students.

The park ranger who had addressed the student group the previous day looked tired and drawn. He was recapping events for the benefit of the new arrivals. The two missing students had been at the northern end of the fire line. The main body of the fire had travelled east and south. The wind had spread the fire, starting multiple smaller fires, some to the west, above the fire break. Firefighters had been quickly deployed to fight those fires because of fears that a fire to the west would rapidly gain momentum and become an out-of-control bushfire if it was not contained immediately. In the confusion of redeploying firefighters to that fire, the fire on the eastern side of the mountain spread further south than had been originally planned by the National Parks staff. The firefighting efforts had been complicated by the need to round up all the students and get them to safety. Valuable firefighting time had been taken up by getting the two injured students up to the carpark to wait for the ambulance. One student had minor burns and the other had a deep gash on his hand where he had fallen over a rock. It was during the rescue of those two students that a volunteer firefighter had also been injured. Once it was clear that Karah and Ava were missing, the State Emergency Service had been called in to assist.

The ranger indicated the approximate area where Karah and Ava had last been seen. In the smoke and confusion of the rapidly spreading fire, no one had seen which direction the girls had gone. The fire had burned the entire area where the girls had last been seen, and on down the slope.

'We don't know whether we're doing a rescue or a retrieval at this stage. Make a solid line and proceed down the slope. If possible, try to cover an area at least fifty metres either side of the spot the girls were last seen. Take full water bottles. Stay in touch with each other verbally up the line and use the radio if you need me. All clear?'

❋   ❋   ❋

'Evander.' Evander raised his head and saw Ben coming towards him. He was desperate to get back to town, to be with Rhea.

'Can you uncuff me, please? I'm not dangerous and I'm not going to do anything stupid. My daughter is missing, and I've got to get back to my wife. She's out of her mind.'

'You're not Elise's dad. What are you talking about? Another missing girl?' Ben's face was mystified.

Quickly Evander explained why he'd come to Snake's old home. He wanted to see if he could find Elise and solve at least one of his problems. He said he knew he'd acted rashly and regretted it now, especially as the discovery of Tobias' unconscious body looked very bad. Evander went on to explain how Karah was missing with another member of her university excursion group, and the fire. His voice caught as he said he didn't know whether his daughter was alive or not, and he remembered Rhea's anguish. He knew she would be more upset not knowing where he was.

'You have to believe me. I just got here a couple of minutes before you. Just long enough to find that guy and I swear he was out cold when I found him. Bleeding from the head and a whole lot of gravel all over the floor.'

'Well, tell me this: do you know who he is?'

'No. I've never seen him before to the best of my knowledge, and that's the absolute truth.'

Some of Evander's sincere anxiety seeped into his words, making them believable to Ben.

'Well, look, mate. You've acted without thinking and it's just got you more worry. I suggest you take some serious notice of what I'm saying. Go home. Be with your wife and sons. Stay there. Please don't go anywhere else. We DO need to question you and your sons more about the activity at the garage and also about this little excursion of yours. I hope good news is waiting for you about your daughter. Are you taking on board what I'm saying?' He undid the handcuffs as he spoke.

'I won't mess up. Thank you for believing me. As soon as I get home that's where I'll stay. Unless I get advice that Karah is hurt or worse. I'll have to go to her.'

'I understand. But let us know, please, if that happens. Now, get back to town and your wife.'

Evander carefully manoeuvred his car around and bumped

roughly over a weedy garden bed before rejoining the sloping driveway.

* * *

Elise scanned the road for further activity but quickly found it a boring exercise when no other vehicles came by. From her vantage point, she surveyed the country all around. Facing the west with the road on her right, she let her eyes drift to her left. *Wait, is that another house further down this driveway? Maybe someone is there.*

She made a quick decision. Down she climbed off the roof, leaving her bag of bricks, but taking her plastic drink bottles with her. She went into the shed and retrieved a couple of hessian bags to stuff in her 'shoes' instead of wet grass. She harvested all the produce she could find and washed it. She stowed her food, including many walnuts and apricots, in her curtain carry-cloth and tied it to the stick to carry over her shoulder. She tied her curtain sarong into a sling, placing her two water bottles and her camouflage curtain inside. She hoisted her sling and her food and left the house, turning south down the track instead of heading back up towards the road. *I'm not really in any hurry so I may as well check out this place in case someone lives there. It's probably only a couple of kilometres and I'm getting pretty good at this walking gig.* The paddocks still had that forlorn air of abandonment, but everything looked fresher after last night's rain.

*　*　*

Mr and Mrs Carlton had aged since Eric's accident. Grey bags showed beneath their eyes, and they moved with fearful hesitancy in the unfamiliar hospital environment. Their cheeky boisterous son lay unmoving, a confusing array of tubes attaching him to various machines. The nursing staff quietly went about their tasks while the bewildered couple sat on either side of the bed. Feral couldn't stand it. He hated to see his brother this way. He hated having to take charge of his parents. They were like a boat without a rudder, drifting without direction, unable to make any decisions on their own. He thought of Snake as an irresistible force who usually acted first and thought after; who took on the world without fear; who was a loyal friend and a cruel enemy. *What the hell had Tobias been talking about, saying Snake had kidnapped a woman?* He'd tried to reach Tobias that morning to try to get some more information, but Tobias wasn't answering his phone. Feral had worried all night, replaying the brief conversation with Tobias. *Had Tobias found the woman? Had the police found her? What had Snake been doing, going to Sydney? Was the woman with him?*

*　*　*

Ava stumbled downhill through the thinning scrub, longingly dreaming of a hot coffee followed by a hot shower followed by a warm bed. She felt desiccated after yesterday's flame-heated wind and sleeping on a bed of bark and leaves hadn't helped. A kangaroo crossed in front of her, veering away in sudden fear when it spotted her. She watched it leap away and realised she had left the thickly forested mountainside behind her. She could see ahead of her a gentle grassed slope. Scanning carefully, she was relieved to see a fence crossing the slope about five hundred metres ahead of her. Her pace quickened. She heard an engine and scanned left and right. Her knees weakened in relief when she spied a vehicle off in the distance, probably as far again away as the fence.

Even though the grassed slope looked smooth, the vegetation hid many ditches and holes. It took Ava another fifteen minutes of tripping and stumbling and half-running to make it to the edge of the road. Not being familiar with how to scale paddock fences, she had made a mess of it and now bore a number of lightly bleeding scratches, but in the excitement of arriving at the road, she barely felt them.

She decided to follow the road as it wound on its slightly downhill course, rather than head uphill. She wasn't sure but she thought she *might* be on the road the bus had taken them on yesterday and going downhill would take her closer to town and to help for Karah. Determinedly, she started walking.

Her persistence was soon rewarded.

Dudley Toukley was driving from his farmhouse to his second block further up the road towards the mountain. He lived a simple and solitary rural life, working hard in the daylight hours and usually too tired at night to do anything other than fix himself a meal and go to bed. He seldom watched the television news. His ancient radio had stopped working one day, and he hadn't bothered to repair or replace it. From the smoke, he had known there was a fire on the mountain, but he vaguely recalled hearing one of his mates in town saying there were hazard reduction burns planned so he hadn't been unduly concerned. He knew he had done all the fire preparation he could on both his main farm and his other block. He didn't have any stock on the mountain block at the moment so that was another reason he wasn't worried about the fire.

He drove calmly, thinking of the work he had planned for the day. Suddenly, he squinted ahead. He slowed down and stared in horror. He was being flagged down by a wild-haired female with dried blood on her face, arms bleeding, skin and clothes streaked with black marks.

'Help me! You have to help me!' Ava reached through the open window and grabbed Dudley's arm.

'Steady on, girlie. What's your problem?'

Ava's words tumbled over each other in her relieved rush to explain. Poor Dudley wasn't used to women, certainly not women who looked like this one did. But he wasn't a hard-hearted man, and he realised this woman was in great distress.

After many interruptions where Dudley stopped her for clarification in the confused torrent of Ava's narrative, he finally had the gist of her problem. 'Gee, love, you've had a rough time. Get in and I'll run you into town. Have you had anythin' to eat or drink? I've got me lunch 'ere and a full water bottle.'

'Ohh, thank you! You're a lifesaver. I'd love some water.' As she spoke, Ava ran quickly around the front of the ute and jumped in. 'I'm Ava. Thanks for the drink. Have you got any biscuits?' She realised her blood sugar was getting low and couldn't bear the thought of passing out now she was so close to safety. Besides, she looked sideways at the farmer; she wasn't sure how he would handle a fainting female. She had the feeling her appearance had rattled him.

'Nah, love. Don't eat biscuits. But I've got a couple of corned beef sangers. I put sauce on 'em. Have one of them if you like.'

Ava hungrily started on one of the sandwiches, feeling only a tiny twinge of guilt at eating the man's lunch.

Relief at being rescued hit Ava. She began to cry, great gulping, noisy sobs.

'Come on, love. You'll be right. You're safe now.'

Gradually, Ava's sobs steadied. She sniffled. Having nothing else, she wiped her face with the back of her hand, straightened her shoulders and helped herself to another drink of water.

'I'm sorry about that.'

'Be in town soon, love. About fifteen minutes.'

CHAPTER 19

Away up the mountainside in Mount Kaputar National Park, the search for Karah followed its methodical course. East of Muswellbrook, another search was in progress. Police, together with State Emergency Service members, were scouring the deserted farmland, looking for any sign of Elise.

In the Nester household, a different type of search was taking place. This search was more of the soul, as the family sat down together and began the long overdue process of clearing the air.

When Damien and Christos arrived at their family home, they politely thanked Cleo for taking care of their mother and firmly suggested that this was a time for the family to be together. Evander had never explicitly detailed to either of the boys his animosity towards the Lardner family, so they didn't ask her to leave out of spite, just from a natural desire to keep family business within the family. Even Rhea had failed to make the connection that Cleo was a member of the family Evander hated so strongly. Realising that she could do no more for her friend, Cleo was happy to leave her in the care of her family.

As she drove towards her home, her phone rang. She was delighted when the caller ID showed it was her daughter, Sophia. 'Darling, how lovely to hear from you!'

'Mum, this isn't a social call. I'm at work. Tobias has just arrived at Accident and Emergency with a head injury, I'm afraid.'

'Oh God, no! Oh dear. I was on my way home. I'll come straight to the hospital. I'll see you there.'

Sophia met her mother in the emergency ward. Tobias was still being treated for his injuries. Sophia said it was likely that he would be kept in overnight at least for observation of his concussion.

'You wait here, Mum. I can't take too much time off my shift. I've spoken to the doctor, and he'll let you know when you can see Tobias. And he'll let you know how things stand with Tobe.'

'Do you think he'll be okay?' Cleo's voice wavered.

'Mum, he should be fine. He's had some sort of blow to his head, and it needs stitches. But I'd say by the look of it, the worst he'll have is a headache for a few days. They've x-rayed his head and there's no fracture.' She spoke with the detachment of a professional, overlaid with a sisterly casualness for her brother.

'Okay. I'll just get a coffee and wait. Thanks for letting me know, sweetie. I'll give you a buzz or text when I've spoken to the doctor.'

Sophia gave her mum a quick hug and a kiss and returned to her duties.

* * *

Having made her decision to explore the possibilities offered by the next distant farmhouse, Elise set off briskly from the abandoned farmhouse. In a short time, she was approaching the house she had seen in the distance. She was in the habit, now, of looking carefully at the ground for fresh tracks or other clues that might indicate recent human presence. She was surprised to see that another unsealed road headed west, parallel to Bees Hive Road. Lying in the grass was an old, weathered signpost saying "Muswellbrook 38".

Good grief! This road goes into town as well. If no one lives in this house, I can follow this into town. That'll keep me safe from Van Man. But thirty-eight kilometres? If it's still that far into town, how far have I walked?

The few days Elise had spent walking and isolated from all the common comforts that she took for granted in her life, felt like an endless torment. But the aftereffects of her cleansing shower, her restful sleep and her filling breakfast had left her feeling energised. Boldly, she pushed open the garden gate of yet another dilapidated farmhouse. To her disappointment, this one was, like the previous two, empty. And, like the other two places, this one also yielded edible produce which Elise promptly harvested. Unlike the other two houses, this one was locked. She had no second thoughts about smashing the laundry window out the back and gaining access. In the kitchen, she washed a head of broccoli, two ears of corn and a large handful of snow peas and added them to her growing food sack. A quick exploration of the rest of the house revealed that the previous tenants had left at least half a roll of paper in the toilet. *Gold!* That, too, was added to her supplies. Back outside, Elise looked at the sky. She quickly decided not to waste any more of the day and resolutely turned her face towards Muswellbrook. *I wonder if I can walk four kilometres in an hour. If I can do that, in seven hours I could cover twenty-eight kilometres! That would leave just a short hop and I'd be back in civilisation. I've got enough food to easily last two days. All I've got to do is find water but at a pinch I could get by without any extra. So, I don't really need to find a farmhouse to sleep in. Just step it out and sleep under the stars. Woohoo, get walking, kid!*

✳ ✳ ✳

'Mum, do you know where Dad is?' Christos asked his mother, sitting down on the lounge next to Rhea and Millie. Her fragile composure disintegrated, and she started crying again, arms wrapped around Millie, face pressed into her golden fur. He looked helplessly at Damien. 'Try ringing him again.'

Evander's phone rang in the car as he sped back towards town.

'Dad! Where are you?'

'I'm on my way home, son. Where are you? Did you get bail?'

'Dad, we're at home with Mum.'

'Oh, God! Has there been word about Karah?' Evander couldn't disguise his panic.

'Not that we know of. Will you be long?'

'I'm about fifteen minutes away.'

'Look, Dad, things are a mess here. Mum's breaking down. We need food for her.'

That reminded Evander that he'd left the house without eating and suddenly he felt hungry. 'Right. I'll grab something. That'll add another ten minutes. Just keep comforting your mum. Tell her I'll be home soon.'

Arriving home with a box of pastries, he walked into the same doleful house he'd left. Rhea was sitting on the lounge weakly crying. Millie, by now, had crawled into Rhea's lap. Damien and Christos wore faces pinched with tension and uncertainty. Although his stomach was a mess of nervous strain, Evander realised someone had to take control. He walked over and took Rhea in his arms.

'Now, love,' he spoke firmly. 'This is no good. We can't

fall to pieces when things get rough. We're all here together and we can support each other. We have heard no news about Karah, so that's got to be good news. There is a massive search party working now to find her.' He seriously hoped he was speaking the truth. 'What we need to do is sit down together, have a meal and pull ourselves together. There are some other things we need to discuss as a family, as well as being together for Karah.'

Rhea had stopped crying. She felt like her old husband was back, taking charge. She stopped feeling rudderless and bereft. She wiped her eyes and fell into the role she had so easily filled all these years. She blew her nose, took a quick detour to the bathroom to wash her face and headed to the kitchen. She hustled Millie out into the garden and filled her bowl with grits. 'You'll be okay out here, sweetie.' She gently stroked the loyal head.

Back in the kitchen, she busied the family. 'Christos, set the table. Damien, see to the drinks, juice or coffee. Stressed as we are, I don't think we should be into alcohol until there is something to celebrate.' While she spoke, Rhea took out a couple of serving plates. She couldn't bear takeaway containers on the table and quickly transferred the pastries onto her own plates. She briefly wondered what the 'other things' were that Evander said they should be discussing.

To his credit, he had a sudden late realisation that the topics to be covered were mostly challenging and unpleasant so he had decided they would not be broached until everyone was well-fed and comfortable.

* * *

'Hey, boss.' Ben beckoned Kaylee. 'We've got the best available team on the job looking for Elise. What say you and I go interview Tobias? The hospital will surely have patched him up by now and I don't want them discharging him before we can pin him down. Slippery little chap has shown he's pretty good at evading us.'

'Ben, that's a good idea. I'll just get that stuff we bagged for Forensics while you hand over. We can drop it off at the lab when we're in town.'

In a short time, Ben and Kaylee were heading back towards town. Ben said, 'I hope Evander has finished with his half-thought-out ideas and is content to stay home now. I guess he's got his plate full worrying about his missing daughter. I don't want to be unsympathetic but at least he'll be getting a bit of an idea what Elise's parents are going through if he had anything to do with her kidnapping, which I doubt now. I've never had such a messed-up investigation. I guess his wife might have a bit of an eye-opener about the garage being closed, too. So all that might keep him busy.'

'Look on the bright side. We're in the process of shutting down part of a car-stealing business. And surely, we must be getting close to finding Elise, poor woman. Tobias might have a little gold nugget for us.'

Cleo had just been briefed by the doctor and told she could see her son. He had several stitches to the head wound and would be kept overnight for observation. He was on pain relief and, the doctor said, should keep quiet for a few days.

Quietly, Cleo approached the bed. 'How're you doing, son? What happened to you?' She kissed his cheek.

'I got hit on the head ...' was all he managed before the two tall police officers walked in.

Cleo assumed they were there to investigate the circumstances of Tobias' injury, mentally casting him in the role of victim. Following the conversation between her son and the police, she soon realised her error.

'Well, Tobias,' Kaylee began, 'we finally catch up with you. You have led us on a bit of a dance, so you can understand we are not very happy with you.'

'In fact, Tobias,' Ben cut in, 'we are quite fed up with your tricks and not at all in the mood for you to try to dodge or mislead us. Do you understand?'

Tobias nodded. 'Mum, do you want to wait outside?'

'Not really, son.'

Tobias grimaced.

'I thought you were a victim, but the police don't seem to be treating you very gently at all, so I'd like to listen and see where this conversation goes.' Cleo spoke firmly, pleased with her new-found confidence. Her curiosity was piqued, and she realised she might be about to gain some insight into what Tobias got up to when so many of his peers were sensibly employed.

Kaylee turned to Cleo and introduced Ben and herself. 'I assume you're Tobias' mother, Mrs Lardner.'

'Yes. Call me Cleo.' She made herself comfortable in the only chair.

'Tobias, can you tell us what you were doing in an abandoned farmhouse on Bees Hive Road?'

Cleo's eyes widened. There was the sound of hurriedly approaching footsteps and Hadley was well into the room before he registered the presence of the police officers. His mother, watching his face, was interested to see that this was an unwelcome sight for him. 'Hello, son.' She smiled at him, offering her cheek for a kiss and effectively stopping him from leaving.

He kissed her perfunctorily and started blustering. 'Soph rang and told me Tobe was in hospital, injured.'

'As you see, she was right, Hadley. And as you can also see, the police are here visiting him. And in a very short space of time, I have gathered that they are not thinking kind thoughts about your brother. Please stay, dear. You may possibly be able to assist the police if your brother can't.'

Hadley's face wore his characteristic heavy frown, overlaid by concern. He moved over to the window.

'Ah yes, Hadley,' Ben said smoothly, 'I'm sure you will *both* be able to help us. Fill in the blanks for each other, so to speak.'

'Who came up with the idea of kidnapping Elise Dean?' Kaylee was tired of making no progress and dived straight in.

Cleo's face lost some of its calm interest. The questions continued from each police officer. If Tobias was hesitant, they turned to Hadley, and where Hadley couldn't answer, they asked Tobias. Kaylee was satisfied to have much of their speculation confirmed by the answers supplied wearily by Tobias and Hadley.

'And, humour me here, Tobias. Did you meet up with Snake at the cemetery to plan this kidnapping?'

Tobias, stunned at the extent of their knowledge, could only nod. Rewarding as all the information was, Kaylee was deeply disappointed to realise that Tobias honestly had no idea where Elise was.

'So, Eric "Snake" Carlton is the only person who knows whether Elise Dean is alive or dead? Is the only one who knows where she is? And Snake is in a coma in Sydney.' Ben's frown was growing deeper and deeper.

Tobias said a quiet 'yes' because all the nodding was making his head throb.

Cleo was now deeply concerned. She was not in the least enjoying the revelations about how her sons passed their time.

'And Hadley, yours was the brilliant idea to hinder a police investigation by encouraging your brother to leave town, was it?'

Hadley nodded, finally coming to the slow realisation of the extent of his stupidity as well as that of Tobias. He knew now they were both in serious trouble. Belatedly, it dawned on him that he was supposed to be the head of the family since his father's death.

'What were you doing climbing over log piles on a farm near Wheeler, Tobias?'

Tobias jumped on a chance to try to reassure everyone that Elise was not dead. He quickly explained Snake's plan of dumping Elise's body there. His mother paled and covered her mouth with her hand.

'How was kidnapping Elise Dean going to stop the investigation into your family? You know she is not a one-woman operation. Her partner would take over from where she left off.' Kaylee was having trouble believing the stupidity of the whole plan.

'Why was that woman investigating our family?' Cleo felt her interruption was reasonable.

Hadley groaned. 'I think Lex's girlfriend's family, the Nesters, initiated it. I think the father thought we weren't good enough for her.'

'Good grief! How utterly ridiculous! Her mother is a great friend of mine. Lex's girlfriend is missing, too. In a bushfire. Lex has gone up to help in the search.'

All eyes turned to Cleo. The two police officers' faces showed their surprise at Cleo's revelation.

'Don't Mr and Mrs Nester talk to each other? How can the father think your family are no good and the mother is your good friend? Seems very odd to me.' Kaylee looked hard at Cleo.

'Not our business, boss. We should just arrest these two, arrange for a police guard on this room and get on with our search for Elise Dean.'

Cleo felt a slow anger begin to burn as the full extent of her sons' criminal activity hit her. 'I cannot say how deeply mortified I am that you have brought this shame on our family, that you have shown such terrible disregard for a fellow human being. You are both a disgrace. I am leaving you to the police but there *will* be a family reckoning, make no mistake. So, you think hard about that while you are in custody.'

Cleo rose with as much dignity as she could and left the room. Once out in the corridor, she quickly called Sophie. 'Do you have a break coming up? I need to talk to you.'

The conversation detailed the revelations Cleo had discovered. She expressed her anger and disappointment at her two oldest sons, saying that from now on, she intended to take an active role in running the tattoo shops. If Hadley and Tobias were in prison, they wouldn't require an income, so she was taking over the business bank accounts, closing her sons right out. If they were not in prison (which she suspected was highly unlikely) she would give them a small allowance and force them to become productively employed members of the community. It occurred to Cleo to think back on Nathan's death. She quickly banished it from her mind. The coroner had found no suspicion of foul play, so she was in the clear. It was now her decision to take a hands-on role in the family business, manage the tattoo parlours as well as develop her budding condiment business. She would become the family matriarch, in the best sense of the title, and put an end to all the drug business and double-dealing. She would make the name Lardner a name to be respected in the community. Sophie assured her mother it was a well-made decision. She added that she had no need of any financial assistance from the tattoo parlour income. Said that, in fact, she was happy to have no part of it. She suggested that while Lex was still a student, he might need a little financial help. The two women agreed that the plan was a solid one to go forward with. Cleo said she'd tell Hadley she needed her signature added to the bank accounts so she could take care of things while he was unable to. And then later, she would quietly remove his signature and that of Tobias and add either Lex or Sophie.

'Well, sweetie, it's been a long morning. Thanks for being a wonderful supportive daughter I can be proud of. I guess you'd better get back to work. I'll call Lex and see how he's getting on.'

Mother and daughter embraced and Cleo left the hospital.

CHAPTER 20

The Nesters had finally talked themselves to silence. Poor Rhea had processed shock after shock. Her thoughts abruptly halted as she realised that she was thinking ahead, making plans. She discovered she was stronger than she thought. Evander seemed intent on turning his life around. He seemed to have a renewed determination to be again the loving head of the family he had once been, if he escaped prosecution for the car theft and rebirthing. With him to support her again as he always had, Rhea felt she could even come to terms with the loss of her daughter if it came to that. Despite the turmoil and lack of sleep, Rhea could feel a new strength and decisiveness flowing through her. She had a sense of purpose at last, after drifting so aimlessly when the children no longer needed her.

'How long will the police have the garage out of action?' she asked. 'The sooner we can get it operating again, the better. But with Snake so very ill, and Damien and Christos barred from working there as part of their bail, you're going to need to hire at least a couple of staff, Evander. I will take over the pawn shop, but it will be a lot less pawn and a lot more quality used goods and certainly no fencing stolen goods. Evander, you're going to have to call your contacts and make it clear to them that they'll have to look elsewhere. I will not be tainted by illegal activity. We will probably have to tighten our belts. I imagine rebirthing stolen cars was quite lucrative. From now on, we'll have to live on what we have earned HONESTLY.'

'I get that, love. I really do. No more illegal anything. No more secrets and no more family feud.' Evander's voice was humble, his words sincere.

'We can do this. We can turn everything around. With some good legal counsel and if we can get the matter dealt with in the local court, the boys are probably only looking at a couple of years inside or a big fine.'

'Mum, I'm afraid it probably won't be dealt with in the local court because we were getting the cars from Sydney. The police said it could be up to ten years in jail.'

Rhea felt her shoulders sag, then she stiffened her back. 'It's your first offence, we'll get a good lawyer. Let's be positive. Anyway, if you're well-behaved in prison, and if you've any sense at all, you *will* be, they'll let you out early. You'll still be young men and hopefully smarter, wiser men. You can always study in jail these days. I've heard some people get degrees while they're doing their time.'

She stood up. 'We've got some big changes ahead of us but so long as we stay a supportive united family, we'll be fine. There is just one point which I will *not* be swayed from. There is to be no more family feud rubbish. Karah can date whomever she likes. Cleo will remain my friend. Evander, I'm sorry but you will just have to accept that. Now, I think we all need some lunch.'

As she walked into the kitchen, her phone rang, showing an unknown caller ID. Face pale, she answered it timidly.

'Hi Mum, it's me. I'm safe.'

'Oh my baby, my baby!' Rhea could hear the sob in her daughter's voice and immediately felt her own eyes flood with tears. 'She's safe! Karah's safe!' she yelled for Evander and the boys to hear. They rushed to the kitchen. She put the phone on the benchtop and switched it to speaker.

'Where are you, sweetheart?'

'I'm in hospital, in Narrabri. They're talking about moving me to hospital in Tamworth. I've badly broken my ankle.'

'Oh, love. My poor girl.'

'I was on the mountainside all night by myself. When they found me, darling Lex was with the searchers. He's with me now. If I have to go to Tamworth, he'll follow and stay there to be with me. I've seen Ava, she's okay. The fire went right over me. Ava was lost too but she ran to the side of the fire and escaped. I ran in front of it and it overtook me. A farmer found Ava and took her to town. She's got a huge bump on her forehead, and they had to stitch it. She'll probably have a black eye.'

Rhea forgave the slightly jumbled account. She admired

that her daughter had been through such an ordeal and was still able to think of others. It didn't escape Rhea's attention that Karah was saying in a roundabout way not to bother coming up, that she was being looked after by Lex. Rhea was happy to leave it to Lex. If he lived up to Karah's expectations in this situation, it would prove the relationship was strong, not just a passing fancy. If Karah had to stay in hospital for any length of time, Rhea was fairly confident it was only a short hour or two drive to Tamworth for a visit. She and Cleo could make the trip. She could telephone her daughter as often as she liked. Now that she knew Karah was safe and didn't have any life-threatening injuries, she felt she had enough to occupy her at home without dashing off to her bedside.

'When will you know if you have to go to Tamworth?'

'Hang on, Mum ... Sorry, what was that?' The listeners in the Nester kitchen could hear that someone was speaking to Karah.

'Oh, right. Okay, thank you. Mum? I'm here again. Yes, I'm going to Tamworth Hospital.'

Rhea spoke decisively. 'Right, my girl. It sounds as if you're in good hands. Now listen to me. I happen to know you were on a day trip, so you've no nightwear, no toiletries, none of the things a girl needs. I also know you've hardly any money. So, I'm laying down the law to you. Your dad and I will put money into your account to be used on whatever you need.'

'But, Mum ...'

'No buts, my girl. I respect your need to be independent, but this is an emergency situation and if your dad and I can't help you out in an emergency, when can we?' She met Evander's eyes and he nodded.

'Okay, thanks.' Rhea could hear that Karah was crying again and she could hear someone murmuring words of comfort.

'Give Lex a list of what you need and he can buy it for you. Actually, put him on the phone. I want to talk to him.'

'Mu-um.' It came out as a protesting two-syllable word. But she handed over the phone because Rhea heard a tentative male voice saying a soft hello.

'Hello dear, I'm Rhea, Karah's mum. Thank you so much for being there for my daughter. I'm putting some money in her account. I guess she'll have to trust you with her PIN. You can buy the things she needs. Do not listen to her telling you to be economical! Buy her whatever she needs, plus a treat if you see something you think she'll like. Are you doing okay? Does your mum know where you are?'

'Yes. I told her this morning. When you and Karah finish talking, I'll call Mum and let her know Karah's been found.'

'Yes, you do that. Nice talking to you. I hope soon to put a face to the voice. Can you put Karah back on?'

'Sure. Goodbye, Mrs Nester. I'll look after Karah.'

'Mum?'

'Sweetie, you've been through a terrible event. Stop trying

to be tough. Accept the money. Accept the loving support of Lex. Being weak now doesn't mean you'll be forever weak. All too soon I know that strong, pigheaded daughter I love will be ruling the roost again.' She was rewarded with a watery giggle. 'That's better. I love you.'

'I love you too, Mum, and thanks. I better give Lex his phone back. Mine's flat. Ring me soon.'

'I will darling. Take care.'

❋   ❋   ❋

'Oh Bill, I think I'm going crazy. I just can't sit here doing nothing, not knowing where Elise is, whether she's safe or not.'

'Shh, love. The police are doing all they can. They're very good at their job. Remember what a success their investigation into Burt's neighbour's murder was? They know what they're doing. Why don't you call Gisella and tell her we'd love to come to lunch tomorrow? It'll be a change for us. I always enjoy catching up with Burt. And you can get busy this afternoon cooking something to take for the table. That'll take your mind off things for a bit.'

'That's an idea. I'd like that.'

In a short space of time, Gisella had learned her invitation to host a luncheon the next day had been accepted. In among crowing with delight at the prospect of entertaining, and sympathising with Bill and Sharon about Elise, she and Sharon worked out what Sharon should bring.

'Come any time after eleven. Will be so lovely to see you.'

Gisella then lost no time contacting Jan Buckley and delegating what food items she was to provide. Then she called Susannah, invited her and Silvio to join them, instructed her that she *must* bring baby Oliver, not leave him with one of his many loving babysitters, and told her what to bring for the meal. Gisella was a force to be reckoned with when she got going.

'First thing tomorrow, Susannah. You help me.'

Susannah smiled. She knew she would not have to lift a finger except to keep the baby in Gisella's sight while she bustled around in her element, preparing a mountain of food.

'Ah, Burt. Happy day. We have everyone here for lunch tomorrow. Big party. Will be good for Sharon and Bill. Take their mind off worry for Elise. Poor girl. Wonder where she is. I get cooking now. We'll have a feast and enjoy seeing each other. You need beer? I can get Silvio to get some from Wheeler.'

'Steady on, steady on. I'm okay to drive up there one-armed, no cops out 'ere. But I'm only makin' one trip. So ya better take a breath and sort out what ya want. I'm not runnin' back and forth because ya forgot somethin' or other.'

Burt grumbled but he was secretly pleased at the prospect of having good friends and a well-catered lunch, and a leisurely afternoon. Gisella clapped her hands excitedly and began writing her list, giving Burt many verbal instructions about what alternative to get if something wasn't available.

* * *

Cleo felt in need of some peace and quiet after she left the hospital. She had a lot to work through, many revelations to be processed. One way and another it had been a stressful morning. She drove downtown and parked outside a café that was a favourite. Its speciality was chicken tacos. She found a table in a quiet corner and ordered, adding a rocket salad and a glass of prosecco to go with the tacos. Just as her drink arrived, her phone rang. Pleased to see it was Lex, she answered quickly. 'What's news, love?'

'Karah's been rescued, safe.'

'Oh, my boy. I'm so happy for you. How is she? How are you? Tell me everything. And then I have a little to tell you.'

Their conversation took the whole time it took for Cleo's food to arrive. She was very sorry to hear of Karah's injury, but pleased and proud Lex had taken control and was staying with her. She was reasonably sure the university would not frown if he stayed away from classes while Karah needed him.

'How are you off for money? I know you keep a very tight budget, son.'

'Okay, I guess.'

Hearing the hesitancy in his voice, clever Cleo knew

that he was worried about affording the upcoming expenses without the income from his job, not that it paid much anyway.

'I'll put some money in your account and then you just let me know when you need more.'

'Mum, you don't need to ...'

'Sweetie, it's no problem. You've got enough worries on your hands without fretting over money.'

'Okay. Thanks Mum. What did you mean you had a little to tell me?'

Cleo launched into a detailed description of all that had happened with Tobias and Hadley, including how Karah's family fit into the narrative.

She concluded by saying, 'I'm taking over running the tattoo parlours and I'm freezing Hadley's access to the bank account.'

Lex was stunned by his brothers' behaviour, appalled to hear they had been part of a kidnapping. He couldn't believe Karah's dad had been so suspicious of him that he hired an investigator to check out his family.

'Wow, Mum. What a mess. Karah and I will have heaps to discuss in her boring bedridden hours!'

'Well, whatever you do, son, don't make any judgements. Don't let all this family business, from your own family and from hers, influence your relationship. Crises like this are wonderful opportunities to see how we each handle things.

Use this to find out each other's strengths and weaknesses. I believe in you, dear.'

'Thanks, Mum. I'd better go. The phone has had a workout, battery getting close to dead. Are you okay with all of this?'

'Yes.' Cleo paused and thought. 'Do you know? I *am*. Very okay! I'm happy to be taking control of the family business and having something to focus on. I'm just very concerned for that poor missing woman.'

'The police will sort it, Mum. Take care and stay in touch. Thanks for the cash. Love you, Mum.'

'Love you, too. Bye.'

*   *   *

The positive effects of her stopover from the previous night remained with Elise. Having seen the signpost that gave her an accurate idea of how far from town she was, she was fired with enthusiasm to make a solid day's trek towards rescue and home.

Elise strode on, guessing that her body was becoming fitter and not suffering at all from the absence of her usual diet of takeaway food, alcohol and baked goods. She looked with interest at the paddocks as she walked on, taking frequent stops for snacks and drinks. The countryside still had the air of abandonment, still no livestock, no cultivation in the fields. Needless to say, no vehicles passed by on the road.

Now, let me see. What day is it today? They took me on Tuesday evening. I slept the night at that first farmhouse. Then Wednesday night I slept by the roadside. Thursday night, last night, I was at the place with the apricots. Thank goodness for all those thrifty farmers and their willingness to put in the extra work to maintain fruit trees and gardens. They've kept me alive. So today must be Friday. Huh! I've jammed a lot into that short time.

*   *   *

'Oh, gee, Ben. We've achieved so much and yet we still aren't any closer to finding Elise. What more can we do?'

'Boss, it's not like you to be discouraged. We've got the best of the best out there scouring the farmland round where we found Tobias. They'll keep going until it's too dark to see and then resume again at daylight tomorrow. I guess the only thing we can do is that task you always love: paperwork.'

Kaylee made a face. 'Yeah, well after the arrests we've made, there sure is a mountain of that! But it's a terrible anticlimax to be just doing boring paperwork. I wonder how Elise is doing. If she could access water, she should be alive. But where is she?'

'I think we can safely conclude that Elise is free to move about. We're almost positive she was dumped at the farm. Snake didn't have a chance to share with Tobias where he took her, but he also seems unlikely to have gone out there and moved her again that Tuesday night. We found her shoe there. She can't be far away. And she must be smart enough to turn on a tap. We know there's water in the tank. I have a strong hunch she's okay. It's just a matter of us finding her. Maybe she is afraid her captors have come back and she's hiding. Tell you what, boss. Let's put in a solid afternoon on this paperwork, then we can go to the pub and kick back with a schnitzel and a couple of beers. Tonight's their trivia night. That'll take our minds off this case. I think we've earned it. Will clear our heads. Even though we haven't found Elise, we've made some significant inroads into other crimes in this town.'

'True, Ben. Okay, you've got a deal. Paperwork followed by the pub.'

They bent their heads to the task and very little conversation passed between them for the rest of the afternoon. Finally, Kaylee closed her laptop. 'I'll meet you at the pub at six, Ben. That'll give us time to order a drink and a meal and be on our second drink in time for the start of trivia. You'd better have your general knowledge brain firing on all cylinders.'

'Why do I always end up carrying the load? What's wrong with you bringing your game brain for once?'

'Hey! Who correctly answered the final question winning us the game last time we did this?'

'Okay, okay, see you there.'

They enjoyed the evening. The trivia night was an entirely different form of mental exertion from crime investigation. Ben and Kaylee were both very competitive and relished pitting their wits against each other to be first with the answer and trying to make theirs the winning team. They teased each other mercilessly, laughing at each other's lame jokes and effectively banishing the case from their minds for a few hours.

CHAPTER 21

True to the plan, all available hands were back on the job searching for Elise first thing Saturday morning. When it came to a human life, no one begrudged missing a Saturday morning sleep-in or early tee-off on the golf course, or breakfast at the markets after a wander around the stalls. Having exhausted all possible areas around Snake's old home, the decision was made to assume that Elise had left that area and started walking towards town. A perfunctory search was made of the road further east of the farmhouse but showed no evidence of anyone passing that way, vehicle or pedestrian. The search party spread on either side of the road and swept slowly towards town, methodically searching for any sign of her. They were looking for bare feet tracks, since Ben had told them Elise was unlikely to have anything on her feet. They had no way of knowing that she had fashioned her own makeshift cloth shoes which effectively smudged her footprints.

Ben and Kaylee were both back at the station energetically wrapping up the last of the paperwork from their rash of arrests, buoyed up by a relaxing night out and a win at the trivia. Kaylee was inwardly seething with impatience to find Elise. She was satisfied that nobody other than Snake knew where Elise had been dumped. She decided to call Bill and Sharon to see how they were coping. Each day, someone from the station had called them with a short negative update, but Kaylee felt that perhaps a personal call from her would be appreciated. As well as that, she wanted to get a fuller idea of what sort of person Elise was, and get all possible clues as to how she would respond to being in her current situation.

'Hello, Sharon? It's Kaylee Bradshaw from the police. How are you?'

'Well, Kaylee, to be honest, I'm not doing too good, really. Just sick with worry and with not knowing. I guess you haven't any news.' Sharon sounded tired and dispirited.

'I understand, and I appreciate your honesty. I'm sorry I haven't any good news for you. Can you answer a few questions for me about Elise, that might help us?'

'Anything, anything that will help. We just want our girl back.'

'We're still actively searching, don't you worry. We'll find her. What is Elise like? Level-headed? Practical? Does she panic?'

'Oh, she's a calm one, our girl. Determined, independent. Good at problem-solving. That's why she decided on being an investigator. She can look at things sideways and see a solution. She's smart, for sure. I know she'd have been scared at first but so long as she wasn't hurt, she'd soon start working out how to sort her situation.'

'So, she'd have been able to figure out which way was back to town, do you think?'

'Oh, yes, definitely. She spent a lot of time at Croham with her cousin, Silvio, when she was younger ...'

'Is Silvio her cousin?' Kaylee interrupted, remembering his involvement in a murder case a while back.

'Yes, nice lad. His dad's my brother.'

'Oh, yes, I remember Burt, too.'

'Anyway, those two kids rambled all over the valley and halfway up the sides whenever we visited, fearless pair. It was always very easy for her to get herself clear about which way was home, using the sun. Why are you asking these questions? Do you know where she might be?'

'I don't want to give you false hope, but yes, we have an idea about where she was left. We found one of her shoes in an abandoned farmhouse about fifty-five kilometres east of town.'

'Oh my god. So far away?'

'We have a huge search party scouring the area. If you're sure she'd have been able to orientate herself, I think it's safe to assume she is headed back towards town. Do you think I'm right?'

'Yes, I think that's a fair guess.'

'But there are only abandoned farms out that way, so she'd have found no one to give her a lift back to town.'

'Oh, my girl! My poor girl!'

'We're fairly confident she has escaped from any ties that were binding her hands or legs, so she'd be free to be fending for herself. Please keep your faith in her ability to survive on her own. Have you got anyone in the family visiting you today to help you keep your spirits up?'

'We're going out to Burt's for lunch. Can't have been much fun for you, that investigation into Felicity Hathaway's murder. Silvio and Susannah gave you the run-around. Gisella is such a lovely woman. It'll be good for us.'

'Yes, indeed it will. I remember Silvio and his folk, in fact that whole investigation as well. You just keep your phones with you and switched on. That way we'll be sure of contacting you if we have any news. Keep believing. We'll find her for you. Goodbye, Sharon.'

'Thanks, Kaylee. Goodbye.'

'Why were you asking all those questions?' Ben's curiosity was piqued.

'I think we can shorten the search by going from farmhouse to farmhouse, rather than scouring the entire countryside. Elise sounds like a resourceful girl. Maybe she didn't stick around waiting for rescue or for her kidnappers to come back. Maybe she decided to walk back to town.'

'So why haven't we seen her on the edge of the road?

There's been no shortage of traffic out there since we followed Tobias and Evander there.'

'I don't know. Maybe she's traumatised and is hiding, fearful that her kidnappers are coming back. Get in touch with your team leader out there. Tell him to split the team. Keep one-third sweeping the road and bring two-thirds towards town to the first farmhouse they see. Scour that one and then move on to the next.'

❊   ❊   ❊

Elise had followed her plan to walk as far as she could in the day. She had snacked and walked through the countryside that still had the forlorn air of abandonment. As the sun was dropping close to the horizon, she had not worried that she hadn't seen another farmhouse. She was quite confident she was heading towards town. She made herself comfortable for the night in a grove of trees that had soft grass growing around their bases. Once again, she had been grateful for the fact that walking made her tired and she slept well. She woke at daybreak to the sound of magpies, butcherbirds and kookaburras welcoming the day with their song. It took her no time at all to have yet another snack and a drink. She was happy to have the walnuts because they were more filling than raw vegetables. She enjoyed a couple of apricots and was once again on her way.

She was so intent on simply making it back to town that

her thoughts went no further. She had yet to realise that she had no clue of anyone's phone number, being totally reliant on the contacts list in her phone. She hadn't planned where to go. She hadn't thought about the fact that she presented a rather strange appearance, with her unkempt hair, her homemade shoes and carrying her belongings in a sling. She simply walked on, so accustomed to the activity by now that she didn't even find it as boring as she had at first.

*   *   *

At Croham, Gisella was swirling animatedly around in a vivid caftan. 'Come in, come in. Ahh, Sharon, you poor mama. Bill, Burt is inside, wanting to see you. Come in.' She dispensed hugs and kisses liberally. No sooner had she ushered Bill and Sharon inside than Jan and Graham drove up and she went through her generous greetings again. She ushered her guests through the house to the long, airy sunroom where the table was spread for a buffet lunch. Jan and Sharon added their plates to the collection.

'Ah, so wonderful have all the family together again. We think all positive thoughts, Elise come home safe, soon. Silvio, make sure everyone has drinks.' She snatched baby Oliver up off the floor and thrust him into Sharon's arms. 'Cuddle baby, always make you feel better. He gorgeous, yes?'

Sharon, well accustomed to her sister-in-law, obediently

took the placid baby on her knees and played with him. 'He's very like you, Silvio. Is he a good baby, Susannah?'

Never at a loss for words when it came to talking about her little son, Susannah sat down beside Sharon and was soon diverting her with tales of his antics.

Burt and Graham quickly involved Bill in a conversation that started with mundane farm matters ('Could do with a spot of rain') but rapidly focussed on the subject that was troubling them all. They each had an opinion to express about the situation, news titbits to be added to the general information, various levels of shock that this could happen in their quiet country region, faith in Elise's ability to make the best of the mess she found herself in.

Finished with drinks duty for the time being, Silvio joined in, thanking Graham for his encouragement to contact the police about 'Trevor Laverty'. The noise level in the room rose as they eagerly discussed everything they knew and speculated on everything they didn't know. Although it was a sad and painful subject for Bill and Sharon, they enjoyed the opportunity to talk about it in the company of loving and sympathetic friends and family.

❋ ❋ ❋

Always hot-headed and impulsive, the effect of his head injury had left Tobias even more erratic and unpredictable. He was subject to sudden fiercely aggressive episodes and angry outbursts. His reaction to any reference to the Nester family was violent and irrational. He and Hadley were out on strict bail and were learning to live with their mother's shocking decision to remove them from their involvement in the tattoo parlours and cut out their association with drugs. Hadley was finding it very difficult to keep Tobias pinned down to the law-abiding behaviour required by his bail conditions. They were to observe a curfew, with no outings after dark. They were not to leave town. They were not to go to pubs or other recreational places. They were to report to the police station each day.

They were driving downtown for their daily visit to the police station when Tobias slowed for a pedestrian.

'That's Evander Nester,' Hadley commented idly, without thinking.

'That bastard!' Tobias shouted. Without warning, he slammed his foot on the accelerator. 'He's the cause of all our problems. I'll kill him!'

The vehicle shot forward. Evander froze, shocked to see the vehicle speeding towards him. There was a sickening thud as the car hit him. Some awful jolting as the big man's body went under the wheels.

'Look out! Stop, Tobias, stop! Stop!' Hadley yelled in despair, hands gripping his head in horror. 'Oh, you fool. What have you done?' It came out as a horrified groan. He wrenched the steering wheel over, veering towards the kerb. They jerked to a halt. People in the street gathered round the inert body. Several could be seen using their phones to call the police, ambulance or just record the terrible scene. Evander's body was twisted grotesquely. Blood was slowly spreading from his head onto the rough bitumen.

'Oh God, oh God.' Hadley could only moan in horror. Tobias sat slumped in the driver's seat, his face deathly pale. The sound of approaching sirens shrilled into the leaden silence.

Attending the scene, Kaylee was appalled at the disastrous turn of events. 'Oh Ben, I feel as if we're totally failing in this investigation.'

'Not our fault, boss. No one had a clue Tobias was so unstable. Maybe he just snapped.'

'What news, Adam?' Kaylee looked carefully at the approaching ambulance officer's face, scanning for an unspoken message.

'Not looking good at all. He has multiple fractures, likely internal injuries, lost a lot of blood from that bad gash to the head. We're in the process of organising an airlift to Newcastle, don't have the resources to deal with such severe injuries here.'

'Oh dear.' She paused. 'All right, thanks, Adam. You get on.' She turned to Ben. 'Tobias is in custody. Hadley can go and wait at the station for questioning. We'll leave the team to wrap things up here and go see poor Rhea. I'm not doing this one alone.'

They were soon knocking at Rhea's door. One look at the faces of the police officers gave Rhea a sick, hollow feeling in her stomach.

'Are Damien and Christos here?'

'No, they're at their place. Evander just popped downtown for some things for lunch. What is wrong? I can see it in your faces.'

'Can we come in?'

Rhea gestured and opened the door wider. They followed her in, pausing to pat Millie, who was sticking like glue to her mistress' side as if she knew bad news was coming. Rhea sat on the lounge and Millie jumped up beside her, pressing close. Rhea absentmindedly put her arm around the dog, stroking her soft golden coat.

'I'm so sorry to tell you this, Rhea. Evander was hit by a car as he crossed the road downtown ...'

'Oh God, no!' Her grip on the dog tightened unconsciously.

'I'm afraid his injuries are very serious, and he's being airlifted to Newcastle. Can your sons drive you there?'

Tears were rolling silently down Rhea's face. She nodded.

'Can we ring them, get them to come over for you?'

Again, she nodded mutely, burying her face in Millie's soft fur. Ben took his phone into the kitchen, put the kettle on and rang Damien to pass on the dreadful news. By the time he had delivered his sad message, the kettle had boiled, and he made Rhea a sweet cup of tea. He took it to the lounge where Rhea was still clutching the dog, asking disjointed questions as her mind skittered over the situation.

'What about Karah? She's in hospital in Tamworth. Oh dear. This is all so terrible. Do you think he'll make it?'

'Rhea, we can't possibly say. He's under the best care right now and will soon be in the best-resourced hospital to deal with his injuries. I'm afraid Karah's injuries will keep her where she is for the time being. Does she have someone with her for support?'

'Yes, yes, um, Lex Lardner is there with her. Oh dear, I can't think.'

'I spoke to Damien, he's on his way over. I told him to pack an overnight bag. Do you want to go and put a few things together so you can get away as quickly as possible?' Ben spoke quietly.

'What about Millie? I can't leave her.' A sob ended the sentence.

Ben and Kaylee exchanged helpless glances. 'A friend …?' Ben couldn't think of anything else.

'Oh yes, of course! Cleo!'

'No, no! That's not …' It was rare for Ben to be so flustered by the emotions of a victim.

'Rhea, I need to tell you,' Kaylee spoke as gently as possible. 'Cleo's son, Tobias, was driving the car that hit Evander.'

A wailing scream broke from Rhea. Millie scrambled to get closer. Kaylee reached for her phone. Ben heard a car in the driveway and went to the front door. 'Rhea. I think we need to call a doctor for you, to give you something to calm you. You've had a huge shock.'

'No! No. No sedatives. I need to be in my right mind.' Rhea made a strong and visible effort to regain control. Stroking Millie seemed to help. Over and over, her hand ran mechanically down the dog's back. She wiped her face with the back of her other hand. She was pale, but she squared her shoulders, reached for the cup of tea. She screwed up her face at the sweetness of it and replaced the cup on the coffee table.

'Okay.' She drew a deep, shuddering breath. 'Well, since you're trained at breaking bad news, can you please let my daughter know what has happened? And I assume you will be in touch with Cleo. Tell her I've gone to Newcastle, and I'll be in touch. I'm *not* letting this damned *stupid* family feud come between us! If the worst happens and I'm going to be a widow, I will need all my friends around me and I *won't* lose Cleo if I can help it. Thank you.' She straightened her back, one hand still resting on the dog. 'Christos can stay here; Damien will take me to Newcastle. As a family, even apart, we will deal with this together. Thank God for telephones. I don't envy you your job. You may go. I have my sons now.' Rhea stood up with quiet dignity and raised her head as Damien and Christos came in followed by Ben.

'Please, Rhea, accept our sincerest wishes for Evander's recovery. If there is any way we can help you, let us know.'

Rhea nodded her head once and the two tall officers left the family to do what they had to do.

'Oh, wow! Ben, that was awful, truly awful.'

'She pulled herself together pretty quickly, though. I think she'll be okay, whatever the outcome is for Evander. She's got her family's support and that's always a big plus. I wonder what the family feud was that she mentioned.'

'I feel sick about it all. Can we grab a coffee before we go see Cleo? She might take the news worse than Rhea.'

Alone in her cool roomy house, Cleo was quite alarmed to see a police car pull into her driveway. Because of recent events, her mind immediately began conjuring up every imaginable bad situation. She prepared herself for the worst and went to the front door.

'Can we come in, Cleo?' Kaylee spoke calmly. She could feel the caffeine from her coffee bolstering her nerves for this latest encounter.

Cleo led the way to the kitchen and stood behind the island bench like a sort of protection from whatever the police had to say. Aside from her hand going to her mouth and the blood fading from her face, Cleo took the news silently. Kaylee carefully passed on Rhea's message about staying in touch. Although she, like the police, didn't understand the reference to the family feud, Cleo was glad Rhea didn't seem to bear a grudge. Realistically, she figured that attitude could change if Evander died. But she felt that Rhea's troubles were bigger than hers at the moment. Tobias was in custody where he couldn't get into any more trouble. Damien could deal with whatever fallout there was from Tobias' disastrous actions. Cleo still had the loving support of her daughter. She resolved to text Rhea and assure her she was there for her but wouldn't intrude unless asked.

Ben and Kaylee drove back to the station. Both were surprised at the resilience shown by Rhea and Cleo.

'For two women who were forced into a degree of submissiveness by their strong husbands, who knew very little of their respective family businesses, who strongly fit the mould of quiet homemaker, both Rhea and Cleo seem to have some surprising strength.'

'Yes. You know, Ben, I think you were right. I think both those women will come through this okay.'

CHAPTER 22

Elise suddenly realised the outlines of the mountains looked familiar. She decided to pause on top of the next hill and thoroughly scan the countryside, looking for known landmarks. Cresting the rise, she was startled to see a house a very short distance down the road. She paused to look around as she had planned, but was stopped on the side of the road for ages because she was suddenly hit by all the unusual aspects of her situation. *What do I look like? How do I get in touch with Mum and Dad or anyone? Where will I go? Who do I tell? Will they believe me or will they think I'm a raving lunatic?*

Marjorie Elton was tidying shrubs in her front garden when she spotted a dishevelled woman standing by the road not far from her house. She watched her for a while. The woman was looking uncertainly around as if she didn't know where she was. She had a bundle in a sling which she put on the ground. She took some food from the bundle and slowly ate, then sipped from a bottle she'd retrieved from the bundle as well.

Marjorie was independent, but elderly. She was aware of her weaknesses, knowing that in the face of trouble, her reactions were neither strong nor fast. She knew the day was approaching when she would have to move to a hostel for the aged. Until that day arrived, she had sensibly decided not to take any silly risks. She felt there was something odd about this woman who was hesitantly standing on the road, absently nibbling the food she'd taken from her bag.

One of Marjorie's safety precautions had been to make sure she always had her mobile phone in her pocket. Slowly she dialled the number for the police.

At the police station, Kaylee was finding any excuse to put off the unpleasant task of interviewing Tobias. She was restless. Her attention sharpened with the ringing of the phone on her desk. 'Yes, Dispatch? What have you got for me?'

'We've had a call that an odd-looking woman has been spotted out east of town, Dhee Road, number 125. Old lady lives alone, not taking any chances with strangers lurking round.'

Kaylee quickly took down the details, feeling her adrenalin rising. 'Ben! Elise might have just walked into town! Let's go!' In haste, the two officers left the station.

In the police car, they quickly covered the short distance to Marjorie's house. Ben slowed as they both saw a woman, standing on the edge of the road, looking doubtfully around. She tensed when she saw the car approaching, then slowly raised her hand. Ben stopped a little way from her, and he and Kaylee unhurriedly got out of the car.

'Elise?' Kaylee called.

'Yes!' Elise suddenly realised she was looking at police officers. 'Yes, it's me. Oh, yes, it's me, Elise Dean!' she shouted. She ran towards the police officers, almost threw herself into Kaylee's arms then abruptly stopped, realising how she must look. Kaylee had no such qualms. She embraced Elise warmly, with both arms.

'You've found your way back to town! So clever! We've been searching for you. How good to see you! How are you? Any injuries? Do we need an ambulance?'

'No! No! No fuss, please. I'm fine. Oh God, Mum and Dad must have been so worried. No, all I want is some clean clothes, a good feed and some shoes!'

'Your parents are at Croham. Gisella is taking their mind off your situation.'

'Oh, sweet Aunt Gisella.' Elise suddenly felt energised. 'Take me to my place so I can clean up and then I'll go out there and surprise them.'

'Okay, how about we take you to your place to clean up? Then we'll get you a feed and you can eat that while we drive you out to Croham and we can debrief you on the way out. I'm not sure you should be driving. That all depends on *if* we think you're correct about not needing the ambulance. We found your blood in the van you were taken in.'

'Oh, that was just a little cut on my ankle. I think it split when they threw me in the van. And I'm pretty sure I'm healthier than I was when they took me!' She laughed a little. 'I've been living on water, fresh fruit and raw vegetables.'

'Ha! I was right about you being resourceful!'

Suddenly Elise's face fell. 'My house! Is it locked? How will I get in? I've got NOTHING with me!'

'We locked it up and have your keys at the station.'

While Elise and Kaylee were talking, Ben walked up Marjorie's drive. He didn't need to knock on the door, the old lady had been watching everything from her garden bench.

'Mrs Elton? You're safe. There's nothing to worry about. That woman was someone we have been searching for, she had been kidnapped. So, you can take some credit for helping us find her. Thank you so much for your sensible precaution of calling us. It's been a good result all round.'

'Oh, the poor thing. I should have helped her, but she *certainly* looked a bit strange.'

'You *did* help her. You rang us. Thank you again.' With a friendly wave, Ben returned to the car where Kaylee was bundling Elise into the car.

'Ben, can you call your team of searchers and tell them we have Elise safe, please? Pass on our sincerest thanks for their efforts. At least they still have some of their Saturday to enjoy.'

'Right. Now, Elise. Where first? Food or clean up?'

'Clean up, please. I can charge my phone while I shower and then I can call Diego and let him know I'm safe.'

'We can do that for you. Let's go, Ben, quick as you like, to

Elise's place via the station for her keys. While she cleans up, you can call Diego and I'll duck over the road and let Mavis know Elise is safe.' Kaylee turned to Elise. 'Mavis saw you being shoved in the van and phoned us straight away. Helpful of her. But I'm afraid even being promptly alerted to your situation didn't help us find you as quickly as we'd have liked. You beat us by finding your own way back to town! We have lots to catch up on.'

They talked non-stop all the way to Elise's place. Although they agreed Elise looked physically well, both Ben and Kaylee were hesitant to take Elise to Croham without evaluating her mental state. She strongly resisted going to the hospital for an assessment, saying there was nothing wrong with her that a proper feed wouldn't fix. 'I'm so *sick* of living on raw vegetables and nuts!'

The two police officers carefully worded their questions to probe for any signs of stress, fear or anguish. They realised that later, as Elise found out the details of her kidnapping and the complex story woven around it, she may have some negative reaction, but so far, all she seemed to want was to be reunited with her family.

Rhea and Damien made good time on the drive to Newcastle. They left the car in the carpark and made their way to the admissions desk. When they asked for Evander, they were shown into a small, quiet room to wait for the doctor. After a brief wait, a slightly built, white-coated doctor arrived and carefully closed the door behind him. 'Mrs Nester, take a seat, please.' He gestured towards the plain chairs. She sat, taking a moment to prepare herself for bad news. The doctor looked very grave. He ran his fingers through his thinning hair.

'I'm very sorry to tell you, your husband died on the way to the hospital. I'm very sorry for your loss.'

Rhea began to cry quietly. Damien sat beside her and helplessly held her hand.

The doctor continued in a gentle voice, 'He suffered a massive trauma to the head, multiple fractures, including ribs. Some of those punctured his lungs which collapsed. I'm afraid he never recovered consciousness.'

Through her tears, clutching Damien's hand tightly, Rhea said, 'That's probably a good thing, he wouldn't have suffered. Oh Evander, poor dear Evander. Poor little Karah. Poor Christos. Oh God, what do we do now?'

'Would you like to see your husband? I can arrange for a social worker to support you. There is no rush to start arranging your husband's funeral. You must take your time to grieve, to start to come to terms with your loss.'

'Yes, I want to see him.' Rhea looked questioningly at Damien, who nodded grimly. 'He was hit by a car, you know. Do we need to tell the police he's, he's ...' Damien's voice caught in his throat.

'I can have the hospital notify the police for you. We will take care of as much as we can, so you concentrate on contacting your family and try to come to terms with your loss. Please wait here. I'll have a social worker here shortly. Again, please accept my condolences.' The busy doctor quickly left to attend to the next crisis awaiting him.

While Elise was taking a long hot soapy shower, Ben and Kaylee waited in her living room. Kaylee's phone rang and she saw that the call was coming from the station. 'Yes?'

'Boss, we've just had word from the Newcastle hospital that Mr Nester didn't survive his injuries.'

'Oh, I'm sorry to hear that. Well, Tobias' charges will have to be upgraded. But he can just stay in the lockup for now. Ben and I will question him when we get in. We're going to take Elise out to her family at Wheeler so we could be a little while. Can you get a detailed account of the incident from Hadley, please? And then I guess you can let him go. Just remind him of the conditions of his bail.'

'Sure thing, boss. Is Elise okay?'

'Yes. She's tired, hungry, dirty but unhurt. She did really well.'

'Happy to hear it.'

Elise bounced into the living room, hair still damp, cheeks pink from the scrubbing in the shower. 'Oh, that was great!'

Ben smiled. 'Diego said he knew people did strange things to get out of work, but this takes the prize!'

'Ha, typical of him!' She grinned. 'Amazing what a difference it makes just to be clean. Now, food! And Croham. That is if you still want to take me?'

Kaylee nodded. 'Yes, of course. We'll take you out there. Your folk will be happy to bring you home, won't they? You don't want to be bothered with driving. You might want to stay at their place tonight, anyway.'

Elise glanced at Kaylee questioningly. Then she realised where Kaylee's mind was going. 'Yes,' she said hesitantly, 'I might be more comfortable at Mum's tonight and have her spoil me a bit. But I'll have to come back here eventually.'

'No need to rush it. See how you feel. Are you good to go?'

More questions followed all the way out to Wheeler, while Elise happily chowed down on a burger, sipping a thick shake. By the time they were driving towards Croham, Ben and Kaylee were satisfied that both mentally and physically Elise had come through her ordeal remarkably well.

They drove through the familiar lion-topped white gates. Gisella, glanced out, frowning. 'Why police come here? Silvio, go see.'

Sharon and Bill shrank together, the joy going out of the day as they were cruelly reminded of their worries. Everyone waited in silence for Silvio's return.

When he walked in with Elise, pandemonium broke out. Ben and Kaylee, following them into the sunroom, had the satisfaction of seeing a wonderfully happy family reunion. Sharon and Gisella embraced Elise in tears. Everyone was talking at once, asking questions, offering food and drink, dragging Elise to a chair.

'I can't thank you enough for bringing our girl back to us,' Bill said to Ben in an emotion-choked voice.

'Don't thank us. She found her own way back. We'll leave you all to catch up and enjoy it.'

Kaylee spoke over the eager questions, 'Elise, we'll be in touch soon. If you start to feel any kind of troubling reaction, don't hesitate to call a doctor or the hospital. You're handling things well at the moment but be prepared for reaction to set in at some point down the track. Remember, you have been through a serious ordeal. But looking at you just now, surrounded by loving family and friends, I think that's the best medicine for you. Enjoy your reunion. Come on, Ben. We've still got work ahead of us. Nice to see you all, Gisella and Burt, Silvio and Susannah.'

Elise glanced around the room before going to hug Ben and Kaylee goodbye. Her gaze fell on the food-laden table, and she said ruefully, 'Perhaps I should have waited before eating. I should have known there'd be a feed fit for royalty here.'

CHAPTER 23

Cleo sat unobtrusively at the back of the church for Evander's funeral, not wanting to intrude on Rhea and her family in their grief. Karah had been released from the hospital but for convenience was using a wheelchair. Lex seemed glued to her side, offering every assistance, and appeared to be comfortably accepted by the Nester family.

As the grieving family followed the casket out, Rhea caught Cleo's eye. She broke from the procession and hugged her friend long and hard, thanking her for being there. 'You and I have a lot of catching up to do,' she whispered.

A couple of months later, both widows continued to take pleasure in their friendship, unweakened by all that had gone on, possibly made stronger. Rhea shared Evander's family feud story so that Cleo could understand what started the whole disastrous chain of events. Cleo was stunned and almost disbelieving, but ultimately it helped her appreciate how secretive of his past her husband had been. Nathan had even controlled what she knew about his past as well as all the other aspects of her life.

Both women were determined to learn the ropes of their respective family businesses. If they were honest, they were grateful to have their time taken up by these duties. They were relishing their new-found independence. Being kept busy this way gave them time to gradually come to terms with the major changes that had taken place in their families.

Tobias was incarcerated pending his court case. He was looking at a prolonged jail sentence for kidnapping Elise and for the murder of Evander. A psychiatric assessment deemed Tobias to be impulsive and immature but not in any way unfit to accept responsibility for his actions. Hadley had been very lucky to get only a good behaviour bond and had recently told his mother he intended to go back to university.

Lex was happily living with Karah at her mother's place, and they had both resumed their interrupted studies. Karah admitted that there were limits to being independent and was grateful for her mother's financial support. Both she and Lex willingly contributed to the domestic funds by paying rent and helping out with household chores. Rhea was happy to have a male in the household for jobs she didn't like doing like cleaning the gutters and mowing. The two women discovered to their surprise that Lex was a creative and adventurous cook. They all enjoyed his Friday evening take-over in the kitchen and Cleo was often invited to share his inventions. Cleo found herself enjoying a closer relationship with Sophia who was very supportive of her mother's move into the world of business.

Rhea grieved for Evander, but the need to adapt to being a businesswoman was a useful distraction. In moments of loneliness, Millie was seldom far from her side. She was a well-behaved companion at the pawn shop where Rhea was following her decision and moving towards antiques and quality second-hand goods. The friendly gentle dog greeted customers, making them feel at home without being over effusive. Millie was also an effective guard dog, showing herself to be adept at sniffing out dubious customers and letting Rhea know. Rhea installed a manager at the garage, kept Feral on staff and employed a mechanic, pending Snake's return to employment. He had eventually recovered sufficiently to be brought out of his coma. Currently, he was undergoing strenuous rehabilitation, helped along by his strong will and upbeat personality.

Damien was jailed for five years for car theft and Christos for three. Both made a commitment to their mother to improve their qualifications while inside.

Elise learned from the police every twist and turn of her kidnapping story. In her turn, she gave Kaylee and Ben an education about survival in the 'wild'. Kaylee was envious that Elise seemed to have shed her dependence on her mobile phone remarkably quickly. Ben was filled with admiration and privately decided to try his own survival skills one weekend. He thought he might invite Kaylee to share the experience.

Following several long conversations with Kaylee, Elise

decided to sell her share of her business to Diego. He said he would concentrate on corporate work. After Elise's experience, he said it made sense to leave the criminal items to someone else. Elise joined the police for on-the-job training in forensics, her degree in criminology being a useful foot in the door. She said she preferred to be under police protection for the dangerous jobs! Bill and Sharon were relieved to learn of her job change. Silvio lost no time telling his cousin she had made the right move.

Elise was once again comfortable in her own home. She made one concession to her personal safety and made an immediate improvement: she built a strong, high-back fence. At the police station, Kaylee was very happy to have someone with proven problem-solving skills join her team. She and Ben continued to work at reducing crime in their town.